The Girl Society

Shelley writes: *To not have tacky sex on your first time, avoid the following:*

1: Doing it in your mother's car and leaving footprints on the windscreen.

At first that's all we've got down. But pretty soon we come up with a whole load of no-nos:

2: Doing it on a sofa.
3: Chewing gum during.
4: Wearing manky old underwear.
5: Bristly legs (on the girl).
6: Dodgy jewellery (on the guy).

We're just getting grossed-out about "7: In your parents' bed" (I mean, eew!) when Mrs Parsons comes in and has a go at us because the bell went ages ago. . .

"Tacky Sex Number Eight," Lia whispers, glancing back at Mrs Parsons. "Excessive facial hair. On the girl." And we all crack up again.

Coming next:

The Lost Goddess

Kelly McKain

The Goddess Society

SCHOLASTIC

For Helen and Laura –
for then, for now, for ever

With thanks to Jane Harris and Amanda Punter for
being great editors and great company, to Joanna
Devereux for your wisdom, support and open-door
policy and to Brett Jones for the roof and the faith.

Scholastic Children's Books,
Commonwealth House, 1-19 New Oxford Street,
London, WC1A 1NU, UK
a division of Scholastic Ltd
London – New York – Toronto – Sydney – Auckland
Mexico City – New Delhi – Hong Kong

First published in the UK by Scholastic Ltd, 2005

Copyright © Kelly McKain, Prospero Promotions Ltd, 2005

ISBN 0 439 96369 9

1

"How can you possibly know what noises she made?!"

We started the Goddess Society on the day Shelley quit school. It gave us a whole lot of trouble – heartache, tears and, in my case, one heel snapping clean off a very expensive (borrowed) Valentino stiletto. Still, we wouldn't change it. Not for a second. Not for anything. Because the Goddess Society made us happier than we ever dreamed possible. And it gave us something else too – see, we started off as best friends, but we ended up more like sisters. And that's for ever.

So imagine this sort of tinkly harp music and the scene going all misty. In case you're not getting the vibe, here's a hint:

YOU ARE NOW ENTERING THE PAST
(Enjoy Your Visit)

Lia and I are in the common room already, both with coffee and sticky buns from the cafeteria, when Shelley comes swaying in, drops her Muji bag on the table and starts telling us the gossip even before she's got her disgustingly skinny backside on the chair.

"So, Carrie's up at the park in her mum's car losing it with Max, yeah?" she says, starting right at the juicy bit. Shelley's only interested in life's juicy bits. "And she's like 'uh, uh, oooo, baby!' and they're really into it. And she wants to come so she shoves her hips up and pushes her feet against the windscreen and starts going, 'Ah, ah, ahhhhhhhhhhhhhh, yes, yes, YESSSSSSS!'"

Lia joins in the orgasm re-enactment while I choke on my sticky bun. By the way, in case you hadn't noticed? I'm not as loud as my friends.

"How can you *know* that?!" I splutter. "How can you possibly *know* what noises she made? Did she *tell* you?"

Shelley looks at me like I'm from another planet. "God, no! And don't let on we know, either! Lucy heard it from Heather who's in the swimming club with Georgie who's Carrie's mate from home."

"So Lucy told you?"

Shelley looks exasperated. "No, Lucy's big sister Jess, when I gave her a lift home from the gym last night," she says, like it's completely obvious. "Anyway, I haven't even got to the good part."

"Oh, sorry to interrupt the narrative flow," I say sarkily, "do go on."

Lia's eyes are popping out of her head by this time

and I can tell she's thinking, there's *more*?

I'm pretending to be above this sort of stuff, but really I'm as keen as she is. I'm probably doomed to lifelong virginity, but still, any info on the subject might be useful. Just in case.

"So that's all great and she's done it and she's really happy, but then the next day she gets in the car with her mum, to go to Sainsbury's, and it's raining. . ."

"Yeah?" says Lia, jiggling up and down as if she's about to pee herself.

"And so the windscreen steams up and these two footprints appear, like invisible ink, on the inside of the glass! Her mum went crazy!"

Lia explodes. "No way!" As her coffee slops, I see she hasn't touched her sticky bun. Huh, the deal was we'd both have one.

They obviously think it's hilarious, but I'm mortified. It just seems so sordid – and with everyone knowing about it as well. And what a way for your *mum* to find out. Yuck! It's enough to send me screaming to the nearest nunnery.

"Poor Carrie!" I say, with feeling. "I don't want my first time to be tacky like that."

"Me neither," says Shelley, pulling an apple from her bag and taking a big bite. Because she's busy demolishing the apple it takes her a minute to realize we're both staring at her. "*What?*" she cries into the silence, spraying juice everywhere.

"I thought you'd done it ages ago," Lia explains. "You know, having your own flat and that. Being surrounded by all those yummy male models."

Shelley looks at me. I look back, *yeah I thought so too*. I thought so because when we were about fourteen there were all these rumours about Shelley and Dan Evans doing it on a pile of coats at Kieran Johnson's party. Lia doesn't know about that because she only moved here about two years ago and, me being me, I never asked Shelley about it – I just assumed it was something she wanted to forget as quickly as possible. I know *I* would. I feel guilty for believing it now.

Shelley crunches her apple more slowly, thinking. Then she pulls out this crazily large Evian bottle from her bag, unscrews the lid very slowly and takes a long swig. This is what Shelley does when she's buying time. "I can see why you'd think I had," she says eventually. "I've got motive, means and opportunity all sorted. But I guess I've just been so focussed on working. If a shoot or casting finishes early, I go and see Stick at the Lily Pad. I meet plenty of blokes, but when would I have time to go out with them?"

"Shelley, you don't have to justify yourself to us," I say gently.

"Yes, you do," says Lia, only half joking. "I mean, all those lush guys going to waste! It should be a criminal offence."

Shelley frowns. "They *are* lush too. On that swimwear shoot with Sam Weston last week I was virtually *drooling*. It's just, I know girls who've got involved with the lads and it's so awkward when it doesn't work out. So I don't even *go* there – plus I'm always busy working my arse off to keep up with this bloody schoolwork – and I'm *still* failing!" She sighs deeply and slumps over her water bottle. "It's official," she groans, "I've got no life."

We didn't mean to bring Shelley down. But it sometimes happens accidentally – like popping a balloon. One minute she's this bright, bouncy thing and then she's just a limp bit of plastic with no va-va-voom. I try to pull her out of it. "You *have* got a life – the sort of life most girls would kill for – getting to wear all that cool stuff and seeing yourself in magazines and all that. And no wonder you're always knackered – you're trying to do almost a full-time job and three . . . two A-levels." Shelley dropped Business Studies just after the February London Fashion Week, when she really ran herself into the ground.

"And it's not *totally* your own place," says Lia. "I mean, it's still in your mum's house, and she's the nosiest person since sliced bread."

"Well, it's not like no one's ever interested," Shelley admits, rallying. "I spent last Wednesday draped round two gorgeous blokes and they both asked for my number."

5

"Exactly," I say. She smiles and hey presto, we're back in Happyland. I reckon I should be a counsellor or something.

"It's time I had some fun," she says. "I mean, all work and no play makes Shel a virgin for ever. Ben and Paul and Sam, look out!"

I agree that Shelley should have more fun, but I'm not sure about all this male model business. We've been to one or two parties with her (literally one or two, she hardly ever has time to go out), and the guys I met seemed pretty shallow to me. "Let's just promise each other that however it happens, it won't be tacky," I say, with feeling.

"What do you mean by tacky?" asks Lia, while Shelley punches buttons on her mobile, checking for messages from her agency.

"Smoking after," I say. "Or smoking before, or during." In case you didn't get that? I hate smoking.

"During?" says Lia, giggling.

Shelley beeps around a bit more, scribbles a few things in her fluffy pink notebook then flips her phone shut. "Let's make a list," she says, turning to a clean pink page.

I reckon Business Studies A-level was a big waste of Shelley's time anyway. I mean, a *list*? The Business Studies kids should study *her*.

Shelley writes: *To not have tacky sex on your first time, avoid the following:*

1: Doing it in your mother's car and leaving footprints on the windscreen.

At first that's all we've got down. But pretty soon we come up with a whole load of no-nos:

2: Doing it on a sofa.
3: Chewing gum during.
4: Wearing manky old underwear.
5: Bristly legs (on the girl).
6: Dodgy jewellery (on the guy).

We're just getting grossed-out about "7: In your parents' bed" (I mean, eew!) when Mrs Parsons comes in and has a go at us because the bell went ages ago.

"And you shouldn't be in here at all, *young* lady," she adds, thinking she's being all witty by emphasizing the *young*.

"No one else minds," says Lia, sort of into her sleeve.

It's true – Mrs Parsons is the only teacher who doesn't get that Lia's like a seventeen-year-old trapped in a fifteen-year-old's life. But we don't want to start her off – technically, Lia isn't a sixth-former, and the last thing she needs is Mrs Parsons launching a full-scale campaign to publicize the fact. As we walk out Shelley flicks her the Vs using her subtle method of pretending to scratch her nose. I slap her hand down because it's not that subtle.

"Tacky Sex Number Eight," Lia whispers, glancing back at Mrs Parsons. "Excessive facial hair. On the girl." And we all crack up again.

Lia scoots off to some obscure GCSE subject like Food Technology while Shelley and I slip in at the back of Media Studies. They're watching *American Beauty* with the blinds drawn, taking notes. Mr Jenkins notices us slide in late, and says, "Nice to see you at last, Miss Green."

He's referring to all the time Shelley's had to take off for modelling jobs. It all started about a year ago, when the three of us were walking along the King's Road, linked arms, going to get the train back to Beckenham. This car screeched to a halt right by us and all the traffic was beeping but this woman didn't bat an eyelid. She got out and just *stared* at Shelley. We thought she fancied her or something, especially when she handed over her card and said, "Call me." Then she had to go because she was getting yelled at for blocking the bus lane. But when she pulled away, giving the bus guy the Vs out of the sunroof, we looked at the card. She turned out to be a model scout. Lia and I weren't surprised. Shelley's six-foot-one, whippet-thin, with long chocolate brown hair and a strong, angular face. It's amazing it didn't happen earlier.

So, anyone would call the number, right? Not Shelley. That's not her style. Instead, she rang the best agency in London and booked herself a go-see. Of course, they went as crazy over her as the first woman and signed her up like a shot. Shelley doesn't mess around with second best. Anyway, at the start of the year, when it looked like she'd be away maybe twice a month, the school were pretty positive about it. But no one had any idea she'd get this much work. Now it's more like twice a week, or maybe even three times (thrice a week?!) – anyway, let's just say the novelty's wearing off.

When Mr Jenkins is looking at the screen, Shelley slips her phone out of her bag and hides it in her lap. She never turns it off – *ever*. I've even seen her taking calls in the *bath*. About ten minutes later, she looks at me with these huge wide eyes and grips the desk. She scribbles something and turns her notepad towards me. It says, "Who needs a man when you've got your phone on vibrate!"

The text is from Lia, who's obviously bored in Metal Engineering or whatever it is. The screen glows in the darkened room: *Tcky sx no 9. Sum1 slaps ur ass and makes tht clickng noise 4 horss!*

Mr Jenkins is cool so normally we don't muck about in Media Studies. But we're already hyped up, so we can't help sniggering like Beavis and Butthead. I feel terrible for being so rude, but I just can't stop myself.

"No one can afford to take phone calls in my class," he says sternly. "Especially not you, Shelley."

Now, if I were in Shelley's Jimmy Choos I'd apologize

to Mr Jenkins and get back to looking all studious. But she's a stickler for detail.

"It wasn't a call, it was a text," she says, without a hint of cheek.

Mr Jenkins gives her a killer look, but lets it go.

And that should've been it, sorted. But then something happens that really isn't Shelley's fault. It's mine. It gets to the bit in the film when Lester and Carolyn nearly do it on the couch. I lean over and whisper, "Tcky sx no. 2," and we both burst into fits.

Mr Jenkins flips like a pancake.

It's not that Shelley got thrown out exactly. It's just that halfway through his speech about how she was crazy for putting a short-term money-spinner above getting an education, something inside her just *went*. I've known her a long time, so I could spot it. She doesn't get angry, like Lia would, or tearful, like me. She just *goes* somehow, and then you can't touch her. It's something I really envy – Miss Emotional Jelly that I am. But it was a shame in a way, because the poor guy was just trying to wake her up to what she was throwing away, and he lost her. Shelley was apparently listening to him with this deeply thoughtful look on her face, like she'd seen the light, and I just wanted to say, "Give it up, sir. She's gone."

So Shelley smiles and apologizes. She says he's right and that she'll make more of an effort and then she picks up her bag and excuses herself for the loo.

Mr Jenkins takes the DVD off pause and probably congratulates himself on saving another young person's future. My stomach's churning, but I get my head down over my notes. And when the bell goes I pick up Shelley's jacket, because I know she's not coming back.

2

"Personally, I blame that vibrating mobile."

I *was* going back into Media Studies, honestly, although I bet Jen won't believe me. It's just that a funny thing happened in the loos. I was staring out the window, feeling really weird and distant, trying to get it together and be *me* again, when a bus went by. So what, you're thinking. But the thing was, the bus had my face on the side. I took it as A Sign. Not in a tarot-reading, crystal-waving Jen-type way. There was nothing mystical about it. It's just that I realized what I had to do. And once I knew, I had to do it right that second. I had to leave right then. Well, I had to tidy myself up first, and *then* leave. I mussed up my new poker-straight layer-cut (I've got this theory that if you get your hair right, everything else will follow) slicked on some Juicy Tubes and went off to find Mr Carpenter, the head.

I *was* going to head straight home after I'd been in to see the big boss man, but I felt all shaky, and I didn't want to face Mum, so instead I'm driving over to the café to look for Stick. I really think he'll understand this.

Stick's got a permanent table in the Lily Pad and he has coffee all day till he's jingling with caffeine and a big plate of whatever the special is at lunchtime. He's one of those annoying people who can eat as much as they like and never get fat, which is why we call him Stick. (I can't tell you his real name, it's far too funny.) I always have to watch the scales and it's really annoying to sit with a green salad while Stick shovels a big pile of sausages and chips into his face.

The Lily Pad's near Kent House station – which is handy because that's where Stick's supposed to get the train to his posh boy's school every day. Instead, at least a couple of times a week, he walks up there and stands on the platform, then when the train comes he nips down to the Lily and e-mails the school office from his dad's account saying he's sick. Stick's thought up some really great lurgies in the last couple of months, but he's on thin ice – I reckon the school are going to bust him soon. They're already hacked off about his floppy dyed black hair, green army surplus jacket and disintegrating school uniform.

The Lily Pad's down a side street and so small you'd hardly know it exists. Apart from Stick, it has a few loyal customers, but Tony, the owner, doesn't actually *want* too many people in. If it got popular, he'd have to smarten the place up a bit or do some actual work. Stick runs his own business dealing old records, working from a laptop and a mobile. Tony lets him work from the Lily Pad because they're both mad record fanatics. When Stick gets something really good he'll always put it by for Tony. Once, he got just the right record to make Tony's wife Lily come back from the fishmonger she'd shacked up with. When he realized how he could cash in on other people's misery, Stick changed his website name. That's how www.thelovemagician.co.uk started.

So, Stick still sells records, but he also sells memories, kind of. He makes money out of people pining for their lost youth, or trying to get their ex-girlfriend back or whatever. He's even had some thank you letters, like, "when I played the record you tracked down for me, it said everything I couldn't say myself, and (whoever) came back to me." It's cheesy, but Stick likes doing it, and he likes the money. It's got so that, sometimes, people don't even want a particular track. They just tell him what's happened, and he gets hold of the right song to fix it. Stick claims to be doing The Love Magician ironically, but I reckon he's a closet romantic.

He looks up and grins at me as I walk in, then finishes tapping stuff into his laptop while Tony does me a coffee. When I sit down, he shuts the lid, a great compliment. I don't tell him I've been pacing up and down outside for ten minutes, my head spinning with this school thing. Instead I just say, "How's it going?"

"Yeah, cool," says Stick. "There's this Nines gig next month actually, the seventh, but all the tickets sold out in about the first hour. Still, I might be able to track a couple down through the net."

"Great. The Nines rrrrock."

Stick's my concert buddy too. It's brilliant that he can afford to do stuff with me. It can be a drag having my own money while the girls are still relying on stingerations from their parents. I'd pay for them too, but they won't have it. At least Jen and her mate Dylan are coming to Tuesday night music club at the studio. It's only three quid to get in and without school to worry about, it might be a laugh.

"The contact I've got in mind might bump the price up, though," says Stick. "I'm not sure if I can afford it."

I smile. Stick can always afford it, it's just that he's got this honour code about how much he pays for things. *Not* a concept I understand.

A message beeps up on his mobile and he grins and turns it for me to read.

I don't believe it, says the message. It's in long hand, so I know it's from an old person. If you want a laugh, watch someone over thirty send a text.

"Believe what?"

Stick just smiles, goes over to the sideboard and unlocks the cupboard. He flicks through his records and pulls out a perfect (1963 Limited Edition) copy of

"Baby Blue Eyes". He snaps a shot of the sleeve and sends it. In a couple of seconds the phone beeps again. *I'll take it.*

Stick flips the phone shut. "Ker-ching."

"Wicked. We're on for the concert then?"

He smiles. "Maybe. How's school?"

He asks me this like a twenty-something looking back, kind of nostalgically, not like someone who should be there right now, doing rugby or Latin or whatever goes on at that place.

"I quit," I tell him, trying (and failing) to make it sound like no big deal.

Stick drops his sugar pack and the grains spill out everywhere. He looks genuinely shocked. "But Shel, what about the directing?"

My stomach plummets. Damn. Trust him to ask me that. I haven't even dared think about it myself yet. I lean forward and blow on my coffee, then pour in a pack of sugar, although I don't normally take it. I stir slowly, while Stick pretends not to notice that my hands are shaking.

"There's loads of time for all that," I say at last, still looking down. My voice sounds strangled, but I press on. "But things move so fast in modelling now. Everyone's always after the new face. It's not the same as in Mum's day, where you could find a niche and stick to it. I've got to make the most of it while the work's pouring in. Besides, I've got no illusions about myself. I

16

know this won't last for ever. I'm not beautiful, just quirky looking."

Stick flinches at that. "You *are* beautiful," he says. I wait for the punchline, but nothing comes.

"Cheers, you're a sweetie," I say, finally looking him in the eye. "But commercially I know where I fit. In a couple of years I won't have the in look any more."

"But it's your *education*," says Stick, dead serious, as if I'm talking about chopping my leg off.

"Ooh. Pot. Kettle. Black. Calling," I tease. "I thought you of all people would understand. We're the same."

Stick takes my hand under the table. I gasp as a hot whooshy wave shoots up my body. God, I'm getting turned on by *Stick* now. Personally I blame that vibrating mobile – it must have had some pervy effect on me.

"We're not the same at all," he says firmly. "I don't really have any other talents. But you do. You can't waste them."

"I won't," I promise him.

He looks at me so sternly we both burst out laughing. "It's purely selfish," he insists, letting my hand go. "The only way I'm ever gonna get on the big screen is if you let me be a waiter or something in one of your flicks."

I feel a rush of excitement. Stick really believes I can do it. He's such a good mate – I just love him sometimes. "You're always letting people relive their good memories," I tell him. "You should be out making some of your own."

"Oh, yeah?" he says, giving me this very un-Stick-like look. "You offering?"

And before I can get my brain in gear, my mouth says, "Maybe."

He leans over the table and it's the weirdest thing but I *swear* he is about to kiss me. Then his mobile starts ringing and he wrinkles his nose, picks it up, leans back.

While he's talking, I stare hard at my coffee, totally bewildered. Half of me is going *what the. . .?* but the other half was about to kiss him back. If there even *was* a kiss to kiss back. I probably just have chocolate powder on my cheek or something.

I think about it all the way home in the car. If nothing else it does an excellent job of blocking out the whole school-quitting drama. *Was* he going to kiss me? I'm always telling Jen to look for the rational explanation, so I take my own advice – and end up with the chocolate powder scenario, although I can't see any now. But I still can't stop thinking about it. Me and Stick? I mean, *hello*. How totally weird would *that* be? We've known each other since that crap youth club we went to when we were twelve. If anything was going to happen, it would have happened *then*, wouldn't it? There's no way it would *now*, we're way beyond that stage.

Anyway, we're both really happy doing our own thing. He doesn't want to get involved with anyone, and nor do I. Not emotionally, anyway. And it couldn't be just physical with Stick – it'd probably all go horribly poire-shaped and I'd lose the friendship. I couldn't bear that – really good mates are hard to find, especially with *my* job. So, by the time I pull into our driveway, I'm totally glad we didn't start anything. If there was anything to start. I wonder if there was? *Oh, shut up, Shel.* God, I do my head in sometimes.

3

"Met any nice boys yet, dear?"

Mum and Dad are pretty cool about me having older friends. They always say, "If you're happy, then we're happy." So actually, they're pretty cool in general.

When we moved here two years ago I did try to hang out with the kids in my year, but after a couple of weeks of the girls comparing boob size and the boys seeing how far they could gob, I was well bored. The final straw was when me and Ryan Beckett spent half an afternoon passing a bit of chewing gum back and forth while snogging on a park bench. Really riveting stuff, huh?

With Shel and Jen it's more like drinking coffee in my room, painting our toenails and *really* talking. We do things like going to the Fresh Spa on Shel's guest passes and getting taxis after parties. When we go out for a pizza we order wine and garlic bread and everything.

I met the grrrls when Shelley's mum dragged them along to my mum's Ann Summers party. They both live in Thornford Road too – Shel's only a few doors down from me and Jen's right at the end, by the block of garages. Shel and Jen had been friends for ages, like, they'd always played out in the street together since Jen came to live with her nan. So I thought they might not let me in. But it turns out, in this case, three is definitely not a crowd – in fact, three is the magic number. So anyway, my mum couldn't just have a normal housewarming party – oh, no. Instead, she reckons the best way to make friends is to invite a whole roadful of strange women to come over and strip down to their Sloggies, then cackle raucously while trying on leather underwear. Weirdly enough, it worked, although I haven't been able to look Mrs Number Twelve in the eye since (I won't go into it, but if I just say it involved a nurse's outfit, one pair of fluffy handcuffs and something called a *black mamba*, I'm sure you'll get the picture – and *what* a picture, eeew!).

Anyway, I got on with Shel and Jen straight away. We had loads in common (i.e. we all agreed that people over thirty should be banned from shagging *full stop*). We sat together all night, giggling and scoffing chocolate willies and not looking at Mrs Number Twelve. It was a real laugh. We've been best mates ever since.

Right now I'm heading to Brambles animal shelter. Before we moved up this end of town and I got in with the girls, I used to help out there every night. Now it's a couple of times a week, but I still love it. It gives me a little bit of cash too (a microscopic bit, but. . .). Cleaning out stinky cages and grooming mangy cats might not be everyone's idea of a good time, but it means a lot to me. Sometimes we get something in – a matted old dog, say – and it's terrified, snapping at everyone, or just going round and round in circles like it's mental. But you keep trying, spending a little more time, cleaning it up, talking to it. Then one day, bingo, you've got this great pet, gorgeous as. . .

Well, gorgeous as my other reason for going to Brambles.

Jase – son of Jackie, the woman who runs it. He doesn't help out much, but he hangs around sometimes, having a laugh with us.

My excuse for going there now is to pick up my coat. I left it in the porch on purpose, so I'd *have* to go and get it. I'm hoping Jase will be in, because I've got something to ask him. I'm trying to make him be there by walking along with all my fingers crossed, going *be there, be there, be there* in my head, which is stupid, but I don't know anything more magical to do – and Jen isn't around to ask.

I walk up the long dusty drive and the lazy creak of the gate sets all the dogs off.

Be there, be there, be there, I wish.

I emerge from the narrow overgrown pathway, and there's Jase, silhouetted in the porch light. He's there, but he's not alone.

22

Hazel.

Now, I reckon being at least nineteen and having a cute little face, long blonde hair and a belly button ring should be *enough* for some people. Hazel can have anyone. Why did she have to go for *Jase*? And she's going for him in a huge way too – a *tongues down each other's throats* kind of way. He's got one hand up her top and the other on her (I hate to admit it, but) perfectly shaped ass.

I raise my eyebrows and, with a bored expression, quip "get a room, guys" as I swish past to get my coat, then swirl out in the manner of someone who has a hot date waiting in a Ferrari round the corner. As I sashay down the driveway I can feel Jase's gaze lingering on my figure, and I hear the satisfying slap of Hazel's hand on his face.

OK, so that's how it *should have* happened. What I actually do is go bright red and stammer something like "gurnunganuuur", then fumble around for ages in the porch to get my damn coat on, while they stare right at me (Jase looking half-amused and Hazel just looking *smug*). Then as a finale I trip on the step and have to run down the drive, pretending I've deliberately gone flying for, like, athletic reasons. I run all the way to Shelley's, pounding my fury into the pavement. If I stop, I'll probably hit something. I did that once – punched a wall. It wasn't the brightest move ever.

Shelley's front door's hanging on the latch (Di, her mum, is totally slack on security – unlike my dad who bolts us in every night) and I steam straight up the stairs to her flat, throw myself in and slam the door behind me. Shel and Jen are deep in conversation and hardly look up as I crash into the studio room (or as Shelley calls it, her parlour-cum-boudoir).

"Bloody Hazel!" I shout. "She knows damn well I fancy Jase."

That gets their attention.

"Uh-oh," goes Jen, and heads for the kitchenette.

I take off my stupid coat and throw it on the bed, catching sight of myself in the mirror. I run my hands through my boring honey-blonde bob, wishing I had long flowing locks like Hazel's. And I've always been proud of my curves, but I suddenly want skinny boy-hips like Shel. God, what's *wrong* with me? Jen comes back with two Bacardi Breezers and a J$_2$O (for her, she doesn't drink a lot) from Shelley's fridge.

I take great gulps of mine in between spitting out bits of the story. I try to make it sound really sordid, the way he was feeling her up, but it's pretty obvious I'd sell my granny to be groped like that. And 'cause Jen and Shel are my best mates, I tell them how it *really* ended.

"Forget him, Lia," says Jen softly, when I finally run dry. "You're better off without him. There are plenty of nice boys at school to choose from."

I give her a look. *"Boys?"*

Jen leans right back on the purple velvet sofa, trying to hide behind Shelley, but I'm not letting her get away with *that*.

"I don't want to go out with *boys*," I say. "Particularly not *nice* boys. Oh my God, Jen, you sound like my great auntie Ethel! 'Met any *nice* boys yet, dear?'"

"Lia, I just meant. . . You know!" Jen starts peeling the label off her bottle to avoid looking at me. "Jason's what, twenty? He's not a. . ." She stops herself from actually saying "kid", but it hangs in the air like a bad smell.

"What are you getting at?" I say.

"If you go out with Jason, he'll expect sex," says Shelley, with all the subtlety of, well, Shelley. "Jen's worried you're not ready for that yet."

I glare at Jen.

"Well, it's not that, it's just. . ." she says, floundering, but I can tell by the way she's blushing that Shelley's right.

"I'm as ready as you two are! Probably more. I mean, God, if *I* was a sixth form virgin I'd have killed myself by now." I know I'm being a major bitch, but I'm pretty narked.

"But it's not the same for you," says Jen, virtually in a whisper. "It's not *legal*."

I can't believe it! I mean, what the hell's *that* got to

do with it? "Look, I'm going to do it when I want to anyway," I say, in a huff. "So you can either be here for me, or not. Whatever."

Shel sighs and swigs her drink. "Of course we're here for you, you mouthy cow!" she goes, sliding down the sofa and poking my thigh with the heel of her boot. "We love you! We adore you! We worship you!"

"OK! OK!" I'm laughing despite myself. "Enough already!" I glance at Jen but she won't meet my eye.

When Shel carries the empties back into the kitchenette I take her place on the sofa and kind of squeeze Jen's arm. "I didn't mean that . . . about that. I was just, like, grrrr. . ." (Apologies have never been my strong point.)

Jen gives me one of her intense looks. "It's only because I care about you, you know?"

I smile. "Yeah, I know. Anyway, what were you two on about when I came in? It seemed pretty full on."

Shel appears and flops into the pink chair, the one with the lovely beaded cushions. "I've quit school," she says. She looks expectantly at me, and after a bit I realize she's waiting for some kind of "what, are you crazy?"-type reaction. I bet that's what she got from Jen. Jen's really into the whole getting-an-education thing. Well, Shel certainly isn't going to get that from me.

"Cool! God, I wish I could just leave that place and get on with my life. You'll have time to really get into

26

your career now. What did your mum say?"

"Not much – she's allergic to anything too parental. She knows I was failing anyway." She glances at Jen. "I'll go to college when the modelling work dries up."

Jen looks dubious, but she doesn't comment. We both know that once Shelley's set her mind to something, there's no way she'll change it.

"Plus, you'll have time to get it on with some of those fit blokes!" I go.

"On that subject, I've been thinking. . ." Shel says.

"Are you sure that's allowed in your job?" I ask.

Shel gives me the fake daggers and carries on. "The first time is, like, a major life event. I mean, you wouldn't just get married without thinking about where it was or who it was with, would you? So why should it be like that with sex? We should make it really special – something to look back on."

I giggle. "What, you want your whole family standing round the bed wearing hats and carnations?"

Shelley laughs along but then goes serious again. You can josh her all you like, but once she gets an idea, she doesn't let it go. "You know what I mean. None of us has done it yet. I suppose if you've got a steady boyfriend it just happens, but none of us have."

"All right, don't rub it in!" I say.

"What I'm saying is, we've got the chance to make it

really good. So, I've got a proposal for you." She leans right forward, eyes gleaming. "Let's form a secret society."

"For what?" says Jen.

"For losing it in a really great way. You know, non-tacky, like we were talking about earlier, at school."

"Yeah, I like it. How about The Groovy Lurve Society?" I say, for a laugh.

"Or the Losing Our Virginity Club," says Shel, dead serious.

"No," says Jen, surprising us both 'cause she's not normally very assertive. "It should be something magical. Something powerful. When I do it, I want him to make me feel like a sex goddess."

"Who's 'him'?" That's Shel, hot on the heels of poss goss.

"No one, just, you know – the guy," says Jen quickly. A bit *too* quickly in my opinion.

"OK, so the Sex Goddess Society," says Shelley. "I like it."

"Let's just call it the Goddess Society," says Jen. "Then we can talk about it wherever we are, without getting embarrassed. . ." We grin at her. "Well, OK, without *me* getting embarrassed . . . and we can call on the goddesses for help."

"All right," says Shel, and writes it down. "Good name, Jen."

The Goddess Society. I like the sound of it too, even

though Jen's reasons are a bit hocus-pocus. She's well into all this new age stuff. Personally, I'm not so keen. Saying that, at this moment I'd happily dance naked around an oak tree at midnight if it would get Jase's hands off Hazel's ass.

I say as much to the girls, and this time Jen doesn't try to put me off. "If it's meant to be, it'll happen," she says.

"If you really want it, *make* it happen," Shel counters.

"How about you guys? Who do you want to lose it with?" I ask.

Shelley shrugs. "Don't know. I haven't drawn up my shortlist yet."

"*Shortlist?*" Jen shrieks. "This isn't a job interview! Jeez!"

Shelley just smiles. She does things her own way, without caring what people think – which is something I love about her.

"What about you?" I say to Jen.

"Oh, no one in particular."

And Shelley goes, "Come on, there must be someone you want to *do*!"

Jen shrugs. "It's irrelevant, because no one's going to come near me in a million years. I've got a serious problem."

For a minute I think she's going to tell us something really *sticky* and *personal*. But then she pulls the side of her vintage flares down to reveal these greying knickers with huge hamster-hammock sides on them. "See what I mean?"

"Oh. My. God." I say, à la Janice in *Friends*. "That looks like a bad case of Tacky Sex Number Four: manky old knickers."

"OK, first Goddess Society field trip," says Shelley. "We'll go into town on Saturday and shop for sexy underwear. But right now, let's make up some rules."

Shelley flips to a new page in her pink notebook with barely disguised relish. I sometimes think she enjoys planning things more than actually doing them. "OK, shoot," she says, pen poised.

"Well, we should be in love with them," says Jen.

Don't get me wrong, Jen's my gorge BFF, but she's so slushy sometimes I could vom all over my shoes. I settle for fake-sticking my fingers down my throat and making retching noises. I think Shel'll join in, but instead she's giving Jen this searching look.

"But how do you *know* when you're in love?" she asks. I just stare – it's like she really cares about the answer or something. Which is ridiculous, because it's well known that Shel thinks falling in love is a hormonal trick to make human beings mate so the species keeps going.

Jen sighs in a really girly way. "Well, it's like, your stomach flips just thinking about the person, and you

30

want to do all kinds of dirty stuff to him, but at the same time he'd go and buy your Tampax in a rainstorm . . . even while the football's on."

Shel frowns. "I hate to break it to you, Jen, but that kind of man doesn't actually *exist* in real life."

Jen just sits there looking all wise and knowing – like she's got the world on a stick.

"God, I don't care about all that Tampax stuff," I say, groaning dramatically. "It should just be someone you *want* with an intense, burning, passionate *lust*. Like me with Jase, for example."

"I'll put a compromise," says Shelley, grinning as she writes something down.

In the end we come up with three rules, and they're all pretty good ones:

The Goddess Society Rules:
1. It should be with someone special, in whatever way that means to you.
2. We'll be sober (or as near as possible without losing the nerve), safe and non-tacky.
3. We'll write about it afterwards and then keep the notebooks unopened until we're really old ladies who aren't getting any and need cheering up.

Shelley grabs a bottle of champagne out of her fridge, one that she swiped from the wrap party for this rock video she was in. She pops the cork and pours the bubbly into three mugs. Jen grimaces and tops hers up with the J$_2$O.

"To the Goddess Society," Shelley toasts.

"The Goddess Society," we repeat solemnly.

"May it bring us only good things, in accordance with the will of the universe," says Jen.

"And may I not be a member very long!" I add, thinking of Jase.

4

"Male models are the way forward."

Jen's nan lets me in, and makes her usual remark, "Ooh, aren't you *tall*, dear?" as if I should be in some Victorian freak show or something. "Video and chocs today, is it?"

Jen's nan is one of those women who have dedicated themselves to growing old disgracefully. But she doesn't do it by dyeing her hair bright orange and wearing wonky lipstick and stuff from New Look. No, that would be playing fair. Instead, she catches everyone off guard by delivering outrageous comments whilst kitted out in pearls and a twinset. It totally works, but I'm determined that today she is not going to embarrass me – so I face her out. As you may have noticed, I can be pretty blunt when I want to.

"No, Mrs Leweston, we've got a Goddess Society meeting actually," I say. "We're all planning to lose our virginity shortly."

Very shortly, I think with a smile, glancing down at the pink fluffy notebook sticking out of the top of my bag.

"Ooh, that's nice, dear," says Jen's nan, eyes twinkling. "It's about time you girls got boyfriends. It's not good for you, sitting around together like a set of old maids. You enjoy it while you're young, poppet. When you get to my age, you'd rather go to bed with Catherine Cookson and a nice cup of cocoa."

I gape at her, feeling my face go hot. She's done it again. Damn. Me – no points. Jen's nan – ten. "I'll do my best," I promise, as I hurry up the stairs.

"Ooh, when my Edward used to take me up the Palais. . ." says Jen's nan, making me hurry even faster.

I throw myself into Jen's room. Lia's already there, and they're both lying on the floor, doing some sort of new age breathing exercise to whale music.

"God, Jen, those American virginity-pledge churches should employ your nan to put teenagers off sex!" I half-shout. "It's verbal contraception!"

As I've obviously wrecked the spiritual atmosphere, Jen scoots up and turns the stereo off.

"Hi, Lia. . ." I say to my motionless mate. Despite the absence of whale noises, she's still spark-out.

"I hypnotized her." Jen waves a book called *Hypnosis for Positive Living* in my face. "She's creating the future she desires through visualization."

I give Jen what Mum calls "one of my looks". Don't get me wrong, I really wish it *was* possible to achieve your goals by lying on the floor with your eyes shut and a huge grin on your face. It's just not, that's all.

"And returning gently back into waking consciousness," says Jen. "Slowly moving your fingers and toes, opening your eyes and sitting up, feeling wonderfully relaxed and refreshed."

Lia opens her eyes and seems genuinely surprised to see me there. "Hi Shel," she says, sounding "wonderfully refreshed and relaxed". "God, that was gorge. I was visualizing my perfect first time with Jase. It was so *real* – almost like being there. Fwoor!"

Jen frowns. "Lia, you were supposed to be doing it for something important, for your future . . . like good GCSE results."

"Sod that!" says Lia, ditching the whole "wonderfully relaxed and refreshed" thing. "Jase *is* my future."

"Look, that hypnosis stuff's got a snowball's chance in hell of working anyway, so why don't you both shut up about it and give me some help," I say, getting my notebook and pen out. "I've drawn up a shortlist of the guys I might lose it with."

Ignoring Jen's look of despair, I read aloud:
"Number one –
Name: Paul Staunton
Age: 19
Hair: Gorgeous floppy brown
Eyes: Blue
Body: Ooooh, mama
Occupation: Model

Car: Audi TT, in silver

Goddess Society Anti-Virginity rating: 100%."

Lia starts dancing around like a cheerleader. "Go, Shel-ley! Go, Shel-ley!"

"God, Shelley, you are seriously scary," says Jen.

"Thanks," I say, and flip the page. "I've got one for you too, actually. Name: Ben Delamere. Age: 18—"

"No, thanks," Jen interrupts, lip curled like I've offered her a verruca baguette.

"Honestly, you should give it a try," I say. "Male models are the way forward."

"Maybe for you. But rent-a-stud's really not my thing. Those sort of boys wouldn't be interested in me anyway."

"Oh, Jen, of course they'd be interested. Look, you can even have Paul if you want. How's that for true friendship?"

"Thanks ... but no," she says, pretty firmly for Jen.

It's a bit of a relief actually. I'm not certain Paul would go for her, or even Ben, if I'm honest. Men like that want to see a bit of lippy. Jen could look really lush if she tried, but she doesn't. Instead, she insists on going round in her mate Dylan's old jumper, which is massive and makes her look like she's trying to hide being pregnant.

"Fine, *I'll* have him then," I say.

"So that's one Paul Staunton, madam," says Lia,

"with extra whipped cream and chocolate sauce. Yummy, yummy."

I put a big tick by his name in my notebook, and when I look up, Jen's staring at me. "You're really going for Paul?" she asks.

"Yup. Why?"

"Well, what about Stick? Isn't he even on the list?"

Lia looks as surprised by this as I do. I blink at Jen for a minute. "Stick? You must be joking!"

That came out much harsher than I meant it to, but Jen caught me off guard. I haven't told them about the kiss. Or the non-kiss, as it was. Or wasn't. Maybe there is something in all these bloody *Develop Your Intuition* books she keeps reading. "I mean, sure, I fancy him in that matey, flirty way," I say, trying to explain how it is with us and totally failing, "but we're talking about my *first time* here. I want it to be the romantic event of the century. You know, serious hunk. Armani suit. 100-quid haircut. Designer stubble. I'd have to wait another five years to see any stubble on Stick!"

"The physical stuff isn't all that matters," says Jen sniffily. The doorbell rings and she moves to answer it, but her nan calls, "I'll go, dear."

"But it matters a fair bit. I'm not saying there's anything *wrong* with Stick . . . it's just, well, skinny white body and three-day-old socks? That's not what I want to look back on when I'm an old granny. And it's not like he's into me that way anyway." The wobble in my voice says, *maybe, maybe not*, but I don't think the girls pick up on it. I plough on, just to make sure. "I mean, we'd probably be in the middle of doing it and he'd leap up and take a call from some Swedish record collector. He'd be more enthusiastic about getting his hands on some rare vinyl than about getting them on me."

Jen holds her hands up. "OK, OK, point taken! It was only a suggestion."

Just then, Inappropriate Nan opens the door. "Someone here for you, dear," she announces, giving me a knowing wink.

Stick hovers awkwardly in the doorway. We all look awkward too.

"Come on in, we're about to watch a film," lies Lia suddenly, all smiles.

"No thanks. I can't stay." Stick turns to me. "I just came to give you something." He opens his hand to reveal two tickets to the Nines' warm-up gig in Union Chapel.

"Oh, brilliant!" I lunge across the room to hug him but he steps back. *Weird.* At first I think he's just staying cool in front of the girls. But what he does next tells me something's really wrong.

He hands me my ticket.

I know it seems like nothing. But he hands me *just* my ticket. What normally happens is that he gives me both. It's our little thing. We pretend it's to stop him selling the tickets on when he gets a tempting offer on the net (which he actually did once and I was furious), but what it really means is that we know we're meeting up for a drink beforehand. That we're going together.

While I'm staring at the ticket, Stick mumbles goodbye and leaves. I look from the ticket to the empty doorway and back again. I don't understand what just happened. Then it dawns on me. He must have heard what I said about him. I mean, who knows how long they'd been standing outside the door before Jen's nan finally stopped eyeing him up and knocked.

"Shel, what's. . ." says Jen, but I'm already running for the stairs. I go clattering down the street, as fast as my silver strappies will allow (the sort of people they're designed for obviously never have to *run* anywhere).

"Hey, Stick, wait up! You forgot to give me your ticket!"

Stick doesn't even turn around. He just keeps walking on up the street. Fast. Shit.

"Stick, I. . ."

He turns then. "Oh, I'll hang on to it. In case, you know, we're doing different stuff." He says this casually, as if we sometimes *do* do different stuff. But the thing is that we *never* do different stuff. Not when it comes to gigs. Then he starts walking again.

I nearly turn my ankle as I dash up the road. I catch up with him again and grab his arm. "What's up?"

He shrugs. "Nothing. What are you on about?" But

I can tell by the kicked-dog look on his face that I was right – that he heard every word.

My stomach lurches. He looks like I just chewed up his heart and spat it out on the pavement. "Hey, come on, I didn't mean it in a bad way. We're mates and that's even better than anything else. I wouldn't want to spoil it and. . ."

Stick shrugs, rocking back and forth in his DM's, examining an empty fag packet by the kerb, while I gabble on. He suddenly looks up and smiles at me. "Don't sweat it, Shel. I wasn't bothered about *that*. It's no problem. It's a bit of a relief you said something, actually. When you said that thing in the café, I thought maybe you fancied me or something, and I was like, whoa. . ."

I just stare at him. I don't believe a word of it. "Stick," I say, trying to touch his shoulder.

He steps back, shrugging me off. "No, really. It's cool. I don't want to go out with a gorgeous model like you – that's such a pathetic male cliché. Anyway, no offence but you're not my type. You're far too sorted. I like my women dark and brooding and on the verge of suicide. And to be honest, I'm glad I overheard how *you* feel, 'cause it makes things easier. See, I gave you just your ticket 'cause I'm going to the gig with someone."

This weird thing happens then. It's like my heart does a bungee jump down to my toes and back again. "With someone, like, your cousin Frankie from Devon," I say, "or with someone, like, *someone*."

40

"Like, *someone*."

I stare. I blink. I open and shut my mouth a bit. Stick's heart isn't in bits on the pavement. He's not even bothered that I don't fancy him. In fact, he's giving me the brush off, big stylie. He's going to see the Nines with someone. *Someone*. Some Little Ms Broody Suicide. Someone who isn't me.

Before I have time to properly *think*, let alone speak, he kisses me on the cheek and starts walking off. "See you around, babe. Cheers for being so cool about the Nines thing."

I am sooooo not cool about the Nines thing, but I say, "Yeah, no problem." I'm talking to his back now, well, more calling than talking, 'cause he's moving fast. "Listen, Stick, I've got that Burberry shoot tomorrow, but I should make it to the Lily by half two."

He keeps walking. "Nah, really can't, Shel. I'm on my last chance at school. If I don't start turning up I'll be out. Then the parents'll kick up big time."

"But see you soon, yeah?" I cringe at my own voice. I sound alarmingly desperate.

"Sure, Shel, yeah." And then he's gone, head down, sloping round the corner in the natural manner of the tall and skinny.

Back upstairs, the girls are like "what happened there?" It's sweet of them to pretend they weren't hanging out the window, earwigging for England.

I sigh and flop down on Jen's bed. "He's going to the

41

gig with someone else. Some girl."

"Aw, mate," says Lia, flopping down next to me in sympathy. "That's the problem with male friends. The minute they get a girlfriend you're dropped."

"Dylan's never done that to me," says Jen. "And it's not fair to assume that about Stick. It could be just this one time."

"Yeah," I say half-heartedly.

I stare at the ceiling, feeling like I've lost something important. But what? I know the girls want me to go into my feelings, but it's hard to actually work out why I'm so gutted. "It just feels so weird him having a girlfriend," I say, sitting up. "It's weird that some other girl might end up knowing him better than I do. That she'll be the one he tells stuff to, and texts jokes to, and *goes to gigs with*." Damn shoes won't come off. I'm fumbling at the straps but my fingers don't seem to be working properly. "It's not a problem. It's not like we were going out or anything. I mean, we've never even kissed."

Maybe we'd never even been *going* to kiss, I think to myself. Maybe. From the looks of things, it doesn't matter any more anyhow. I have this tiny fleeting little thought that maybe I do want to be with Stick after all. That maybe that's why I'm so upset. But I push it out of my mind. If it was Meant To Be (in Jen-speak) I'd have had a lightning realization the moment I met him by that village hall Coke machine, wouldn't I?

42

"You should be happy for him," says Jen, distractedly, staring at my shoes.

"Yeah, I know. What's wrong with me?" I say, finally getting the straps undone and kicking my shoes across the room. Jen flinches for some weird reason, but I don't question it. I know better – she just clams up if you ask her about anything. Honestly, she hardly even wants to tell you what she had for tea. I see that Lia's noticed it too, and give her a look to keep her mouth shut. Then I fall back on the bed and groan loudly. "Why do I feel so shit about this?"

So what do my so-called best friends do? Is it:

A – group hugs?

B – shedloads of sympathy?

Or even C – breaking out the chocolate ice-cream?

No. What they do is take one look at each other and start laughing.

"What? What's so funny? I'm in pain here!"

"Oh, Shelley, you know we really love you and everything, don't you?" says Jen.

"Like, loads," says Lia.

"Don't beat about the bush," I say impatiently.

Jen takes a deep breath. "Well, don't take this the wrong way, but you're just put out because Stick wasn't really upset. You're so used to assuming everyone fancies you. . ."

"Well, they usually do," I say huffily. It's only the facts, after all. "So?"

43

"So it hurts your ego when someone doesn't."

Well, *that* hurt my ego. I wish there'd been a little bush beating. I know I take myself too seriously because I'm all goal driven and that, so I try to laugh along. But I can't. I feel like a slug on a pile of salt.

Lia obviously agrees with Jen, 'cause she says, "Welcome to Planet Earth, Shel. Where rejection is a fact of life."

I'm about to feel even worse, when I suddenly realize what this means. I sit bolt upright and stare at them. "You're right. That's exactly what it is," I say. "It's just my ego thingy not liking the rejection. It's not that I *want* Stick or anything."

Lia looks at me like, *whoever said you did?* And I realize that I had hidden my confusion about the maybe-kiss really well after all. Well, from Lia at least. Who even *knows* what goes on inside Jen's head.

"Instead of being glad that Stick feels the same I want him to sit in a girl-free zone being undyingly devoted to me while I swan off with another guy," I say, marvelling at the sordid way my mind works. "God, what sort of a mentalist am I?"

Jen pats me on the shoulder. "Sounds like you're just an average human being."

"I know how to cheer you up," says Lia. "Lunch, then shopping for gorgeous sexy underwear."

Lunch. Shopping. Just the words make me instantly feel much better.

5

"Life is short - eat dessert first."

We head into town, linking arms with Shelley in the middle. She's wearing really high strappies, which I'm especially thrilled about as it helps the rest of the world notice what a chubby short girl I am.

I love Beckenham. It started off just being a place in Kent and ended up sort of tacked on to London. We've got a tram now, as well as the trains, and loads of cafés and pubs and an arts centre where they have cool stuff like tango lessons and comedy nights. The next thing you know, we'll have the tube and David Blaine in a box and it'll be £4.50 for a cheese roll.

Shelley announces that absolutely the only thing to do for underwear is get the train up to Victoria and go to the big La Senza on Oxford Street. But by the time we get halfway up the hill to the station (about four minutes' walk) we're starving, so we get a table in La Dolce Vita, a little Italian café that does great grilled paninis with loads of oozy cheese. We've hardly sat down when Shelley and Lia start asking me about blokes again. Uh-oh. I thought I'd got away with pretending there wasn't anyone. I hide behind the menu and ask if anyone wants to split a side salad.

"Come on, Jen, there must be *someone*," says Shelley, after the waiter's taken our order.

Thinking on my feet, I go for the "no-one-could-possibly-want-me" bluff. I've been down on myself so often in the past it's totally convincing now. "And even if I did find someone, I'd be far too embarrassed to actually have sex with him," I add, for good measure, "I'd probably do it completely wrong."

Lia and Shelley just look at me, totally bewildered, but the doing it wrong thing really is a worry of mine, so I plough on. "I mean, there are probably all sorts of rules and moves in sex, like, say, in tennis, that you have to know or you can't do it."

Lia smirks. "What, like, get in bed and then whack any balls that come your way?"

They laugh while I blush. "Not the *same* rules, obviously."

"Maybe you should get some *magazines*," says Shelley. I just sit there blinking at her. "They tell you everything," she adds, which is when I realize she means those girls' mags like *Cosmo* and *More!* rather than *Playboy* or something.

"They just freak me out even more! They make it seem as though everyone in the universe knows the finer points of giving a good blow job. To be honest, it was only halfway through last year that I realized *blow job* kinda meant the opposite. . ."

I join in the laughing at that, as if I'm joking. Which I am. Definitely, OK?

Then the food comes and Lia starts noisily sucking up the bits of grilled pepper that are escaping out of her panini, while I pick strings of mozzarella cheese off my chin. We're such a sophisticated bunch. I feel another toe-curlingly embarrassing sex conversation coming on, so I create a diversion by getting Shelley into a debate about the autumn/winter collections, which lasts the whole meal.

When she finally stops gabbling about Marc Jacobs and finishes her tomato, spinach and mozzarella salad (easy on the cheese, heavy on the leaves) about three waiters rush up to take her plate away. Just as the queen must think the world smells of fresh paint, Shelley must think the world is full of wonderful people tripping over themselves to help each other out. When she asks for another bottle of Evian, Lia and I seize the opportunity to order something gooey for dessert.

"Seriously, Jen, you've got to chill out about sex," Lia tells me, picking up the very thread I've been hoping they'd forgotten about. After the blow job hilarity I'm determined to keep my worries to myself. At least she's off the *who's the guy* thing, though. "I don't think it's possible to do it *wrong*."

"I bet it is! OK, maybe not the obvious bit but I

mean the other things." I wrinkle my nose as the four men on the next table all light up cigarettes. "What is this, some kind of sponsored cancerathon?"

"Don't change the subject," says Shelley.

"What kind of other stuff?" says Lia, probably hoping she'll get the chance to do another orgasm re-enactment. The smoking blokes seem pretty interested too, come to that.

I shrug, and take a minute, as if I have to think of something. As if these things don't go round in my head all the time. *As if*. "OK, for example, what if the guy said, *talk dirty to me*? I'd probably say, 'Greasy pans, mouse poo, muddy boots. . .'"

Shelley and Lia crack up – charming, hey?

"Maybe if you get used to talking about sex, you'll be less embarrassed about actually doing it," says Shelley.

The nicotine fiends at the next table are all-out earwigging now, probably hoping for some free phone-sex-style conversation.

"Go on," says Shelley, "try it. What would you like to happen?"

"Well. . ." I whisper. The girls lean in really close and I swear I can almost see the smokie-dokies' ears doing a cartoon stretching thing and landing in our bread basket. "Well, he'd touch me on the, like, you know, well, with his fingertips, really softly, his other hand kind of brushing, well, you know. . ."

"No, we don't know!" Lia explodes, as I trail off lamely. "Jeez, Jen! Don't ever take up writing erotic fiction, will you?" The next table also realize they're not going to get any gratis perv-line thrills from *me*, and start talking again.

"Well, if you're going to take the piss, I won't talk about it at all," I say, in a huff. "In fact, I'll drop out of the Goddess Society and be a virgin for ever. And even if I stay in, there's no way I'm doing Rule 3. There's no way I'm writing about it afterwards."

"Aw, Jen, we're only joking. . ." says Lia. "Anyway, no one has to see what you write except you."

"But that's the thing – *I* don't even want to see what I write!"

"Course you're staying in. We're all in," says Shelley firmly, not letting my comment slip by. She holds up her glass. "To the Goddess Society."

I smile as we clink our glasses together. "The Goddess Society."

A gruff voice above us says, "The What Society?"

We look up and there's Jase, standing over our table, his gross nicotine-stained teeth on display in a wide grin.

"Oh, nothing," I say quickly, silently thanking the universe that we didn't call it the Losing Our Virginity Club. "We've just been debating why we live in such a godless society."

"Er, right."

I've only met Jase once before, but there's something about him I don't like. It's nothing concrete, just a feeling and, of course, a couple of shuffles of the tarot deck that didn't come out in his favour. That's the real reason I don't want Lia to go for him, though of course I can't tell her how I feel.

"Oh, hi, Jase," Lia says breezily, pretending she's only just realized he's there.

"Hiya." He's in the perfect position to get a good look down her top and he's taking full advantage of it. I watch Shelley watching him stare at Lia's boobs, and I can see from her face that she isn't exactly taking to him either.

So I'm thinking, *say something, Lia – slap the pervy git*, but she just puts her elbows on the table and sort of squashes them together even more. The instant Wonderbra effect makes Jase's eyes nearly pop out. And they're naturally a bit boggly as it is. What *does* she see in this guy?

"Oh, er, you've met Jen, and this is Shel," says Lia, finally remembering we're there.

Jase moves his head the slightest bit to grin yellowly in Shelley's direction, then goes back to Boob Patrol.

"Nice to have met you, Jase," says Shelley, as if he's just going. "See ya."

"Hazel not about today?" says Lia, fake-casually, ignoring Shelley's hint.

50

"Nah. Chucked her in."

For a second, Lia's face goes into kid-at-Disneyland raptures, but then she pulls on a look of deep concern. "Oh, poor you. And poor Hazel, too. Breaking up's a bummer."

Jase shrugs. "Yeah, well, you know. . ." He's doing this brave little soldier impression as if he's suppressing some deep and meaningful emotional pain. It wouldn't fool a five-year-old. Which is why I can't believe it when Lia grabs his hands and says, "Oooh, mate, if you want to talk about it we can meet up sometime, yeah?" She catches my steely look and adds, "Alone."

Jase nods. "That'd be cool. Say Monday in the Beast and Burden, about half eight?"

Lia says, "Sure, great," without even a second's hesitation.

I mean, why don't you just take your dignity and flush it down the toilet?

Then Jase does this unbelievable thing, and I can tell even Shelley's thinking, that's it, he'll get a slap now. He runs his finger right up the front of Lia's top, all the way under her chin and slightly tilts her head towards him. I can see how that might be totally sexy, if it wasn't such a moron doing it, in public, in the middle of La Dolce Vita. But Lia's obviously getting the sexy without the moron, because she visibly shivers.

Jase leans in close to her neck and whispers, "Thanks, you're a good girl."

He turns to us and it's clear that the dislike is mutual. "Laters," he says and struts off looking exactly like a peacock that thinks he's God's gift to, erm, lady peacocks. (Quick, give that girl an English A-level!)

"So that's the famous Jase," says Shelley.

Lia nods and sighs, and I swear I can almost see little butterflies and hearts twittering round her head. Well, no, actually – more like little lacy pants and silk boxer shorts.

I raise my eyebrows, but bite my lip. There's no point mentioning the age gap again. The way Lia's draped over the table, with a look of complete bliss on her face, it's obvious that between me and Jase, it's me she'd be telling to take a hike. "Wonder why he and Hazel broke up?" I say, trying to sound casual.

"Oh, who cares? The fact is, he's back in the game, and he wants to go out with *me*!"

Just then, two portions of chocolate fudge cake and one bottle of Evian arrive on the table. Shelley thanks the waiter who takes as much time as possible to fill her glass. He looks like he's about to say something, but then Lia starts talking and he reluctantly slinks away.

"Shel, can I borrow your Lipsy top for Monday?"

"Sure. It'll be a bit tight on you, though."

Lia grins, stabbing her fork into the gooey cake. "That's exactly what I'm hoping."

"Lia!" I go, but she just smiles angelically and says, "Life is short – eat dessert first." Then she shoves the huge forkful of cake in her mouth and dissolves into chocolate-induced ecstasy. I give in, dive into my cake, and join her.

As we split the bill and get up to leave, I realize that I want to be alone. It's not only because I don't fancy trekking into town for another giant dose of embarrassment (although that's part of it). It's just, over dessert I've somehow got into one of my *inner* moods, and it's too late to shake it off. When I feel like this, every time someone talks to me it feels like they've got a little hook and they're trying to pull me out of myself. So I make a big deal of frowning at my watch and saying I promised Nan I'd be back by two to help her wash the net curtains.

"Oh, but Jen," says Lia, linking arms with me and trying to pull me up the hill towards the station, "we all have to go together. Goddess Society rules."

"Yeah." Shelley rummages in her bag and hands me her mobile. "Call her and make something up."

Lia grins. "Or just call her and say exactly what you're doing. Your nan's cool – she'll totally understand how important it is."

But it's no good. I just want to be alone in my own head. So I do a pretty rotten thing. Even before it's out of my mouth, I feel guilty. But that doesn't stop me saying it, I notice, which makes me feel double guilty with extra cheese. "Actually, there are some papers we have to discuss about Mum," I mutter.

"Oh, no probs."

"Sure."

Of course the girls instantly back off. They know I hate talking about this stuff. As they both give me looks of deep sympathy I feel really warm about them being such sweeties, until I remember that there *are* no papers. God, what a twisted person I am, to use Mum as an excuse like that. But then, it does the job – and not for the first time, either.

"We'll pick out something for you too," says Shelley.

"OK," I say, doing my fake brave smile (and there I was criticizing *Jase*). "Just, nothing too. . . You know what sort of thing I'll like."

"Yeah, sure," says Lia, giving me a huge wink. "Leather thong, studded bra, rubber suit, in fact anything remotely kinky. Don't worry, we're on the case."

She's joking. *Isn't she?* Shelley must see the alarmed look on my face, because she says, "Black not red. Foxy not tarty. Silk not lace. . . OK?"

"Yup," I say, relieved, "and as a general rule, choose what you think, then put it back and find something with double – no *triple* – that amount of material."

When we hug goodbye outside the café, both of

54

them give me a sympathetic little extra squeeze which sets the guilt-manufacturing centre in my brain working overtime. I watch them head for the station and when they round the corner I turn and wander down the hill, making for The Beckenham Bookshop. I just want to pick up this lit crit book I ordered for next term, and then go for a mosey in the park. I need to think – to get some stuff straight in my head. See, I've got a secret – and it's got to come out. Soon.

I've never told anyone. Not even the girls. You know what I said about, *oh yeah, right, where would I find the perfect guy?* Well, it's not true. I meant to tell them the truth today, over lunch, but when it came down to it, the mood wasn't right. It's sort of sacred – I couldn't take any jokes about it. And when something's been a secret for this long it makes it almost impossible to say. I mean, I've said the words a gazillion times in my head, and there are quite a few versions written in my journal, but. . .

Well, OK, the truth is that I *have* found the perfect guy. There, I've said it. I've been in love with someone for over ten years, for over half my life, since before I really understood what I was feeling. I have a really vivid memory of the day we met, when me and Mum moved into the big crumbling villa at Darville Road, in Stoke Newington. The landlord couldn't be bothered to do up the flats nicely so we got one cheap. Lizzy came up and invited us down to their place for some tea, then me and her son Dylan spent the afternoon making their tiny linen cupboard into a witches' den. Later, we all went for a walk round Clissold Park and got ice-creams and me and Dylan played a made-up game round the lake.

In fact, it's always been me and Dylan.

That's why I'm going to tell him now. I've been putting it off since I was about fourteen, but I can't hang around being shy and awkward any more. It's about time I turned into a swan. I know I should have said something sooner, but I've sort of been leaving it up to him, although nothing's happened yet. He's probably been just as scared as I am about making a move. You see, I've thought about *us* for such a long time it's become this perfect fantasy, and now it seems almost impossible to make real.

But I *am* going to make it real. I want to lose it with Dylan, and I want to be his girlfriend. But that's not all. I want us to be together for our whole lives, too. I want us to get married and have kids and one of those big pine tables we all sit round talking and eating Jaffa Cakes with homework books and tennis rackets and odd socks all over the place. Then in forty years' time I want to take our grandchildren for an ice-cream in Clissold Park. Is that totally mad?

Maybe.

But it's how I feel so it's about time I said something. Took a risk. That's what my cards say too, and my palm and my stars and my tea leaves (not that I dwell on this subject or anything!).

It's all a bit scary, though, because I've never been out with anyone before. Not even once, not even when all it meant was which boy you put your arm round in the park and who bought you a box of Matchmakers on Valentine's Day. But then, it should be OK. Dylan's never been out with anyone either, well, not seriously. Sure, he had a few little flings at school with those blonde, bouncy, permanently cheerful type girls, but they did his head in after about a week. Under the surface, it's always been *us*.

We're two of a kind.

Imagine the girls' faces! It'll be the Goddess Society virginity-losing event of the year. I'll just waltz in there and say, "Yeah I've done it, with the love of my life, who's also my best friend, and we're going to be together for ever. Coffee, anyone?"

Isn't it weird? After all these years of waiting, I can hardly hold on another second – but I have to. Till Thursday night.

As I step into the bookshop and go up to the counter, I'm thinking, wow, the next time I come in here I'll probably have a boyfriend and maybe, just maybe, I'll be an ex-virgin too.

6

"Is that a python in your pocket or are you just pleased to see me?!"

I take a deep breath and walk into the crowded pub, glancing at the reflection of Shelley's top in the glass door. It goes really well with my new black hipsters from Topshop. I've borrowed her driver's licence too, just in case. I can't believe they'd bother checking ID on a Monday night, but still, the barman asks when I order a glass of red wine (I reckon it's more sophisticated than a bottle of voddy mix, like I normally have). I flash Shel's licence, with my thumb over the date of birth. Luckily the guy only half-glances at it. In this get-up I look at least twenty anyway. He gives me this *sorry, just doing my job* smile, and I grin *doesn't matter* back.

I pay for my drink and look for Jase. He's with a bunch of mates round the pool table. For a minute I feel gutted that he's not on his own, but then I remind myself that this is it – I'm actually here, to meet him, 'cause he asked me. This thought makes my heart start hammering and I have to sit back down on a barstool for a bit and wait for it to calm down. I'm going for *cool chick* here, not *cardiac arrest*.

Jase looks up and smiles as I walk over. I drink in his sandy curls and ice-blue eyes. *Melt* – he's the best-looking guy in the place by far. I'm trying to do that hip-swinging thing that Shelley showed us and not spill my drink at the same time, which is tricky so I just give up and walk normally. I hover by the pool table as he takes a shot on the black. Just looking at his arm drawing back then thrusting quickly forward makes me go all hot. I suddenly feel really thirsty and find myself gulping at the wine, wishing I'd got my usual after all.

As the ball slams into the pocket Jase looks up and winks at me. My throat seizes up and my mouth freezes as I smile back. Jase straightens up, hands the cue to his mate and comes over. This is it, Lia, I say to myself. This is your chance. Do *not* muck it up.

He hugs me hello, lifting me off the floor a little bit. Just being touched by him is so amazing I think I'm going to *die*, but I try to keep calm. I don't want him to hear the hammering in my chest and think I'm not cool. I breathe him in – peppermint chewing gum, some kind of really manly smelling aftershave, Lacoste maybe, smoke and beer. I swear, if they could bottle essence of Jase I'd buy a crateload.

I have to force my smile down a bit. You see Marilyn Monroe do that on old film footage sometimes. She grins like a lighthouse beam and then remembers that it looks mega horsey and tones it down. I pull my lips together and secretly thank Marilyn. I want to look like a sex bomb, not a grinning, dribbling idiot.

"Glad you made it," says Jase in my ear.

He's joking, right? Or maybe he actually *doesn't* know I would've killed all my rellies and climbed over a pile of their dead bodies to get here. "Yeah, thanks for asking me," I manage to say.

Jase gestures for me to sit down on the bench behind a table. What a gent. He slides in after me and is probably just about to say something deeply sexy when some guy comes up to us. He's clutching three dripping pints of lager in his hands and he's got a couple of bags of Walkers clenched between his teeth, which he drops into the middle of the table. For a split second I think he's just a barman, but no such luck.

"This is Wayne," says Jase. "Wayne, Lia."

Wayne puts the pints down and wipes his beery hands on his jeans. "Don't mind if I do," he says and shakes my hand. Which makes it go all sticky. Which I pretend not to mind about. Wayne sits on one of the stools across the table from us. Which I also pretend not to mind about.

Seeing the pints, the guy who Jase just beat at pool ambles over and takes the other empty stool.

I give him a smile, and seeing as we haven't been introduced I say, "Hi. I'm Lia."

Instead of saying his name, the guy just goes, "She

60

your new bird, Jase? Whoor. She makes that Hazel look like a right minger."

What with girl power and all that I know I should act narked off about the Hazel comment, but I can't help being pleased. But then Moron Man does a really obvious double take at my boobs and goes, "Nice rack, too." That's too much. They often do that, don't they, blokes? You're having a laugh and then they overstep the mark.

"Lia, this is Tez," says Jase. "I'm not introducing you, mind. He doesn't deserve to know a nice girl like you."

Tez grins like it's a compliment. "Wouldn't mind getting my head between them," he says, *right in front of me*. "Bet you wouldn't either, Jase, you lucky, lucky boy."

Jase blushes at this, which I think is really sweet, but Tez can go and do one. I bet he's got a dick like a pencil. I give him the Vs using Shelley's patented nose-scratching method. I mean, a girl likes to go out and look sexy and get noticed, but I'm not into being treated like some kind of prozzie. I pull Shelley's top up a bit, finish my drink and pretend to be majorly interested in the promotion on the back of the beer mat.

Wayne tears the crisp bags open and gestures to me, *help yourself*. I give him a grateful smile. He's quite fit actually, once you get past the sticky-out ears and vacant expression. He couldn't get a girl like me though, I think, surprising myself. Maybe some of Shelley's confidence has rubbed off on the borrowed top. Or maybe it's 'cause I'm with Jase. That would make anyone feel like a total goddess.

Jase flicks his Jack Daniels lighter open and lights his fag all in the same movement. I'm well impressed. There's something cool about it, like those people who can shuffle a card deck, zooop, in two seconds flat, or park a car virtually without *looking*. Stuff like that just melts my stomach.

The guys start chatting away and for a while I stay pretty much out of it, ignoring anything Tez says, but nodding along when Jase or Wayne are talking, sometimes dropping little comments in to show I know a bit about football and cars and telly, that I'm not some sort of girly girl. Jase and me are sitting pretty close together, and my heart's still hammering, but at least I'm managing to string a few words together.

That is, until he puts his hand on my thigh.

For a minute I think he doesn't realize, but then he gives me a quick little wink. Tez and Wayne are still chatting away, with no idea what's going on under the table. It feels so amazing – secret and sexy and. . . *Hello*, his hand's travelling *up my thigh*. Wayne's talking about the new Arsenal striker and I'm going "uh-huh, uh-huh" when really I want to start going "uh, uh, uhhhh!!!"

See what I mean about Jase being cool? It's like,

nothing's even been *said* about how we feel, but we just totally *get* each other.

It's a shame when Jase moves his hand so he can have another smoke, but it's also a bit of a relief because I think I'm about to come right here at the table – and this time I won't be faking it. Tez gets the next round in and after another glass of wine, I'm feeling pretty relaxed. I start talking to Wayne and Jase about how I'm hoping to get a nursing assistant job at a vet's next year, and do my nursing course on day release when I'm seventeen.

Jase smiles in approval. "Wicked idea, Li. You're a bright girl. You go for it."

"Yeah," says Tez. "Not like some of these girls that trick you into getting them pregnant so they can get a council flat."

I must look well shocked because Jase smiles at me and says, "Just ignore him. He's not talking about all girls. He's really just talking about Julie, his ex-bird."

I want to ask Tez how Julie could have *tricked* him into getting her pregnant. And I want to tell him he's a total tosser while I'm at it. Things have been waiting to kick off between us all evening. Luckily Jase picks up on the vibe. He reaches into his pocket and, glancing at the free pool table, pulls out a couple of quid coins and hands them to Wayne.

"Do me a favour, mate, and take Tez off for a game,

will you?" he says. "Me and Lia have got stuff to talk about."

Have we now, I think, getting a headrush.

Before Tez can kick up, Wayne drags him over to the pool table. Now that we're alone, at last, I reckon I better get in some pretence of doing what I came for. "So, how are you about Hazel now?" I ask.

"Oh, erm, yeah, fine. To tell you the truth, she did my head in. Always on about where was I, what was I doing? That sort of bollocks drives blokes away."

"Yeah, girls don't like it either. Well, I don't, anyway," I say. "So – happier being on your own, are you?"

Jase looks right into my eyes. "No," he says. "See, I broke up with Hazel because of someone else."

"Oh, right." I look down at the table, flustered, wishing I'd never started playing the agony aunt. The last thing I want to hear about is some other girl he's been seeing. "So that didn't work out either then?"

Jase grins. "Well, I dunno yet. It's you."

I look up sharply, relief and joy plastered all over my face. I know it's a long way back to Coolsville from here, but so what? I'm going to savour the moment. "Me?"

"Yeah. I saw the way you looked at us that night on the porch. You were totally gutted."

I turn my eyes to the table again. I was hoping he hadn't noticed the whole being totally gutted business.

"After that I couldn't stop thinking about you. That's why she started getting all narky, she could tell I wasn't into her any more."

I, Lia Harcourt, do solemnly swear that I will never take the piss out of Jennifer Leweston's new age hoo-ha again. That visualization worked miracles.

"Yeah, you're right," I manage to say, still looking at the table. "I do like you . . . a lot."

Jase puts his hand back on my thigh, which makes me shiver and turn to mush all over again. Even when he moves it, I can feel the handprint still there, burning.

"So, you and me, yeah?" he says.

Damn straight, I think. "If you like," I say, trying to regain some grip on coolness. But it's tricky. I've got the one thing I've been hoping and wishing for since I first saw him at Brambles. Well, OK, maybe not since I *first* saw him. I was still hooked on that Robbie Jones from school then. But pretty soon after. It's enough that I'm not doing cartwheels round the pool table.

"I need the loo," I say. Jase doesn't move. "Seriously, if I don't go right this minute I am going to pee myself."

Jase stretches and stands up to let me wriggle out of the tiny space between the bench and the table. I have to brush right up close to him to get by. I almost do actually pee myself then.

When I get in the loos I wish I'd remembered to

charge my moby, so I could phone the girls. I glance at my watch. Ten past ten. Shit! I did (solemnly) swear to Dad that I'd be back by ten, seeing as it's a school night and all that. He said if I wasn't he'd come down here looking for me. I pop some chewing gum in my mouth too, 'cause I did (solemnly) swear to Dad I wouldn't drink either. He's got this thing about how the landlord could lose his licence if he serves me and I don't want him starting on about it again. He might stop me meeting Jase here, and there's no way I'm letting that happen.

I wash my hands and hurry back into the pub, pausing for a second to admire Shelley's top in the mirror and to grin at myself in a dazed kind of way. *I'm with Jase*, I see the mirror-me mouth, though I'm not sure the real me believes it.

Jase stands up to let me back in at the table and I have to really resist the urge to do a bit of gratuitous squeezing past him. Instead I lean over, grab my bag and kiss him on the cheek. "I've gotta go. I said I'd be back by ten and if I'm not. . ."

"What, your dad'll come down here and drag you home?" Jase smirks, like it's a really witty joke and not something that could happen any minute.

"See you soon, yeah?" I say, striding towards the door. I feel like Cinderella legging it from the ball. Like maybe I should leave him one of my shoes.

Jase follows me and catches hold of my arm. I spin round, overjoyed and annoyed at once.

"Don't go," he says simply.

Overjoyed wins and I grin toothily, then remember to do the Marilyn smile instead. "I've got to. Really."

"I'll call you," he says.

I raise one eyebrow. "You'd better. I don't take any shit from men."

His eyes twinkle as he grabs me and pulls me close, and it's like, *hello, is that a python in your pocket or are you just pleased to see me?*

Then he kisses me. A full on snog, right in the middle of the pub. And whoosh, I'm a rocket shooting into the sky on fireworks night. I explode into a million shards of colour and I just *zing*.

People are staring – but I don't care. I don't care that some guy's got a forkful of chips poised in midair. I don't care that the barman's slowly pouring wine into a glass that's already full. I don't even care that my dad's just walked in wearing his special car coat and frayed old slippers.

God, he's a good kisser.

Jase, not my dad, obviously.

7

"Quick, talk about *Neighbours*!"

I'm standing in my parlour-cum-boudoir working a bit of styling cream through my hair. I'm hoping that my "get the hair right and everything else will follow" proverb will work tonight. I've got my favourite red boots on too, for luck. It's the first time I've seen Stick since that really awkward conversation we had in the street. You know, when I thought maybe I fancied him, because of how I felt when he took my hand in the café? And when I thought maybe he fancied me, because of the kiss. Well, maybe it was going to be a kiss or maybe I just had a chocolate-powder-on-the-cheek situation. Oh, God, I can't start this again – especially now that it's completely irrelevant.

Stick doesn't fancy me and I don't fancy him. Simple. I just hope he's not still in a mood with me. I wouldn't blame him if he was – I shouldn't have been talking about him like that. What I said wasn't exactly complimentary, was it?

Mum pushes my door open with her pink-nail-varnished toes and hovers in the doorway. She does this all the time and it really annoys me. I catch her looking at me and frowning. I pretend not to notice, so she does a little sigh. Then another. Eventually I give in and say, "What?"

"Oh, nothing."

I decide to bluff her. "Oh, OK."

But she keeps frowning and sighing and eventually she can't hold it in any more. "Don't wear that skirt, Shel," she blurts out. "It makes you look fat round the hips."

I resist even turning to look in the full-length mirror. I'm sure I look fine, and I don't want to give her the satisfaction of seeing me doubt myself. I used to get upset about how bitchy she is, and she still riles me, but now I just try to detach and not react. This time I regain control by changing the subject. "Jen's coming over in a minute."

"Oh, good," says Mum. It's so depressing. I mean, I'm the teenager here. Surely I get to be the sarcastic one? "How is Miss Patchouli Whale Music?" Mum continues, with an annoying little smirk on her face. "Still wafting about in those long skirts and baggy jumpers? I don't know why she hides herself up like that – I mean, her figure's not too bad. Nothing a few weeks at the gym wouldn't fix, anyway."

I just roll my eyes and start gathering my dirty clothes into a pile in my arms. Over the years I've learnt that it's easier to handle her if I'm bustling about. That's since I realized that constant bitchiness isn't actually a positive response. I used to act the same as her – well, I was a kid, I didn't know any better. But then I started having problems at school, you know, people I thought were my friends making pacts to ignore me and even a bit of bullying-type stuff. Well, I thought I was always on the receiving end, but I've since realized that what I thought was being funny actually really hurt people. The fact is, *I* was the bully half the time. Thanks a lot, Mum.

Mum frowns at a silk top I've just grabbed from the arm of my purple chair. "That should go in at a lower temperature," she says, going all domestic on me. She lights up a B&H and wanders out into the hall (technically her area) before I can snap at her. I don't have smoking in my flat.

She catches my expression. "Careful, darling, you're getting as uptight as Jen. She's so *self-righteous* – you breathe one puff of smoke vaguely in her direction and she acts like you've sprayed her with poison gas."

I've managed to blank off from Mum so far but that gets to me. "Why do you have to be such a bitch?"

Luckily the doorbell rings. You still have to get into the main hall to get up the stairs to my flat. Mum smiles. "I'll get that. You finish your make-up, love."

I don't say that it *is* finished. She knows damn well it is.

I hold my breath as I hear Jen's voice, but Mum just says, "Hello, love. That's a nice skirt. Go on up."

Mum must know I tell the girls what she's really like. Or maybe she doesn't realize, because she doesn't know she's *like* anything. When I ask her why she has to be catty all the time she just tells me not to be so sensitive. But the thing is, I'm not really sensitive at all. I mean, think of Jen – if she had to live with my mum she'd be a gibbering wreck after about ten minutes. I feel guilty thinking that – Jen hasn't got a mum at all, just a memory. For the gazillionth time I promise myself I'll start making more of an effort to get on with mine.

I hear Jen climbing the stairs and shout, "Hang on, I'm coming." I pull my door shut, lock it (I don't trust Mum an inch) and gallop down.

"I thought Lia might ring us, about last night," says Jen in the car on the way to the studio.

Oh bollocks. I knew this was going to come up. "Yeah," I say, pretending I need to concentrate on the roundabout.

Jen squints at me. "Hang on, she *did* ring you, didn't she? She just didn't ring *me*! It's because of what I said about Jase, isn't it?"

A strange high-pitched laugh comes out of my mouth. "Of course not! Don't be so paranoid! She just had to get down to work, because her parents are getting really angsty about her exams. She knew we

71

were going out tonight so I said I'd give you the lowdown."

Jen doesn't look like she believes it. She shouldn't – I just made it up. It's true that Lia felt she couldn't tell Jen about the date, even though I tried to get her to make the call. I can see that Jen feels left out. I just don't know what to say to her, so I do what I always do in these situations – plough on. "Yeah, her dad was really cross about her not being home by ten and apparently he could smell that she'd been drinking. He even saw her and Jase kissing! But she said she wasn't seeing him any more."

"Good," says Jen, suddenly perking up. "I'm glad she's seen sense. She can't afford to get involved in something like that with her exams so close."

I pull into the studio car park, turn off the engine and stare at Jen. God, sometimes I swear she is from another planet altogether. "She only *said* that so her dad wouldn't give her the third degree and maybe even ban her from seeing him. You know her parents would go mental if they found out how old he is. She's just better off keeping it under wraps."

"But how can she lie like that?"

I shrug. "That's love for you."

Jen raises her eyebrows. "That's lust for you, more like."

I grin. "Come on, lighten up. She's having fun."

"Yeah, that's what worries me."

We get out of the car and clip-clop up the steps and in through the huge Victorian doors of the studio. My stomach flips as I spot Stick, propping up the bar with Dylan, talking music no doubt. I give him a nervous smile and he smiles back. Thank God. My worries melt away. Course there was no problem. Strange, I don't know why I ever thought there would be. We all say hi and hug and order some drinks.

"I hear you've left school, young lady," says Dylan, eyes twinkling.

"Yeah. Best move I've ever made. It's such a relief not to have a pile of work waiting for me when I get home. How's *your* course going?"

"Great, thanks. I'm still working on my songs. The whole thing's been a real eye-opener." Dylan goes to the Brit School, which is a specialist training place for musos.

"When am I going to hear some of these new tracks?" asks Jen.

"When I'm good and ready to play them to you," Dylan replies, winking at her.

Hang on, do I detect *flirting*? Jen and Dylan are always really pally together, though, so it's hard to tell. It's probably nothing – I'm just on red alert because of this Goddess Society virginity-losing thing – everyone's suddenly become a potential candidate for Jen's big night.

"I really wanted to go to the Brit," says Stick. "Shame I've got no musical talent at all."

"Never mind," I tell him. "Bunking off one school's pretty much like bunking off another."

Stick gives me the fake daggers. See, we're exactly the same as Jen and Dylan, and *we're* not flirting.

"Yeah, but where would musicians be without people like you?" says Dylan. "You're a genuine music freak."

"Just a genuine freak, you mean," I chip in. Stick cuffs me round the head playfully and says to Dylan, "If I'm so vital then how about a cut of your profits when you make it big?" The boys shake on the pretend deal. It's great how they get on so well. We've been out like this a few times now and they've really bonded over the local live music scene.

We're just weaving through the crowd with our drinks, looking for somewhere to sit, when I hear my mobile beep. We find an empty table right near the stage and I dump my stuff on my chair and pull it out of my bag. It's a text from Paul, replying to the one I sent about going out on Saturday night. It says, *PCB for 8 OK? C U Zbar 7?* I grin. PCB means Palm Court Brasserie. I've always fancied going there, which I made sure I mentioned in my text. You have to make these things clear to blokes, don't you? Especially as it's going to be my perfect virginity-losing night. I don't want to end up somewhere horrible. Everything's got to be just right.

Stick leans over and for some reason I flip my phone lid down. "Oooh, something you don't want me to see, is it?" he jokes. "Hey, Dyl, Shel's getting dirty texts."

I make myself smile. "Yeah, right, I wish! Actually it was just this guy Paul Staunton, about a shoot we're both in."

I don't know why I lied about the date. After all, there's no reason not to tell Stick. But still, I don't want him to know.

Jen gives me a quick glance and my eyes flicker, *yes it was, yes it's on.* She gives me this weird look – I suppose she's cross with me for lying to Stick. With Lia lying to her parents as well, she must think she's the only one with any standards left. Maybe Mum's got a point about her being a bit self-righteous. Oh, God, I feel guilty for even *thinking* that.

Stick leans over the table towards Dylan and goes, "Hey, look at that fit barmaid."

Dylan's eyes search the bar and fix on a tall slim girl with long black hair. "Yeah, she's lush, but more your type than mine, mate. You ought to watch out, Shel. You've got competition."

"Ha ha," I go.

"So, why *aren't* you two together yet?" Dylan's only joshing us, but I feel Stick tense up next to me. It suddenly seems really awkward.

75

"It's not like that," he says. "Shel doesn't fancy me."

I peer at him. "You don't fancy me either."

Stick grins. "Yeah, well, you are a bit of a minger, to be honest."

I give him a slap and Dylan laughs. "I know why you two could never go out," he says, "you get on far too well."

Jen looks scandalized. "You total cynic! Isn't getting on well what makes a good relationship? Surely that's the most important thing?"

Dylan smiles at her. "Yeah, only joking, I think you're absolutely right." He gives her a lingering look. Maybe I *am* detecting flirting.

Then the band kicks into action and we can't hear each other speak, so we stop bothering to try. We can hardly hear the lyrics either, the guitars are up so loud, but it doesn't matter. It's just really nice to be out with my mates.

In the break between bands, Stick goes to talk to this guy Danny who occasionally sells him records and Dylan goes for more drinks.

Jen's looking all distant and worried, so I ask her what's up, even though I can already guess.

"It's just this thing with Lia," she says. *Bingo*. "If her parents think she's not seeing Jase, that means we're the only ones who know what's really going on. We've got to look out for her, Shelley. Who knows what he might try on with her."

"It's more a case of what she might try on with him," I say. "You know what she's like."

Jen sighs. "I know what she *acts* like, but I think a lot of it's just bravado. You have to remember, she *is* younger than us. Underneath I think she's quite scared about having sex."

I snort with laughter. "Lia? No way! Now you're definitely projecting your own feelings on to her!"

"Fine, then let's just stick to the facts," says Jen snappily. "She's in the middle of her GCSEs, and she's *fifteen*."

I decide to be straight with her, however harsh it sounds. "Jen, you know I'm not mad about Jase either, but you mustn't go all disapproving on Lia. She'll only get annoyed. Look at the way she didn't phone you after their date. You can't be there for her if she's shutting you out."

Jen looks hurt. "But you told me she didn't call because she had to study."

"Look, all I'm saying is give her a break," I say, more gently. "She's taking control of her life and going for what she wants – surely that's a good thing?"

Jen sighs. "I suppose so. I just wish it wasn't with that idiot."

Jen's gaze strays towards the bar, watching Dylan load our drinks on to a tray. "And while we're on the subject, maybe it's time you started taking control of *your* life," I say pointedly.

"What do you mean?"

I'm not one hundred per cent sure, but acting it is the only way to get Jen to admit to anything, so I take a gamble. "Oh, come on, Jen. Something's going on between you and Dylan, isn't it? You're into him, aren't you?"

Jen looks absolutely horrified, then she gathers herself and takes a deep breath. "OK," she says finally. "Yes, I am. I've been meaning to tell you for a while. It's just been impossible to make the words come out of my mouth."

Yee-hah! She shoots, she scores! "Permission to tell Lia."

"Permission granted. And tell her to bloody well ring me about Jase. I'll be lovely, honest."

I know she's trying to do her subject-changing thing, but there's no way I'm letting her get away with it. Not with gossip *this* good. "So, wow, how long have you felt this way? Have you said anything? Has anything happened? I mean, have you kissed or. . ."

"Shush!" hisses Jen, as Dylan nears the table. "Quick, talk about *Neighbours*!"

So we do. It's the patented worldwide way to pretend you weren't just having a heavy conversation about the person coming towards you.

"Hey, Jen, do you want to come and see the mixing board?" says Dylan. "I might play here soon with some guys from college and I want to check out the set-up."

Jen glances at me uncertainly. "Er, sure."

I give her a wink and a smile as they head off to the side of the stage. Unsubtle, I know, but I can't help it. It's just so cool that those two might get together. I mean, there are friends who it definitely wouldn't work out with – like me and Stick – and friends who it really might. I think Jen and Dylan fall into that category. Stick sits back down and in the spirit of being friends who it definitely wouldn't work out with, I decide it's time to ask him about his date. Maybe I'll even come clean and tell him about Paul. "So, this someone you're going to the Nines with – what's her name?"

Stick looks startled. "Oh, didn't I tell you that before?"

He takes a long slug of his lager and then he's about to say it and suddenly I absolutely do *not* want to know. "No, hang on, don't tell me. . ."

"Why not?"

I shrug. "I don't know." And I really don't. It must be my stupid ego thingy again – you know, that Jen was talking about before. "If it gets to the point where you've got a house in the country and three kids, well, maybe you can tell me then," I say.

Stick's just about to say something when Jen and Dylan come back. Thank God.

Jen's got this flustered intense look on her face. *Hello.* What's going on?

The boys are talking about records, and the room's

buzzing with chatter so I reckon it's safe to interrogate Jen. "Well?" I hiss, leaning into her.

"Oh, nothing like that. It's just, for a minute he got this strange intense look on his face and I thought he was about to say something important. You know, I thought he was finally going to talk about *us*. But then he went all sort of mumbly and said this wasn't the time or the place."

"Ooooh," I go. "He wants to get you alone." I feel a real thrill for her, in the middle of my chest. "Oh my God, Jen. He is going to tell you!"

Jen smiles shyly. "Here's hoping. But if he doesn't, I'm going to tell him."

"What, *now*?!"

"No! But he's round on Thursday night." Dylan looks over at us. "Talk about *Neighbours*!" Jen hisses.

So we do. Again.

The boys fall silent for a moment and Stick catches on to what we're saying. "God, is that all you ever talk about? *Neighbours*?"

"Yep, well sometimes *EastEnders* as well," Jen jokes, sending me a quick little look.

I can't believe it. I mean, she and Dylan have always been close. And of course, he knew Iona, which means a lot to her. I give Stick a big grin as the band starts up again. He doesn't know why I suddenly look so happy. He doesn't know that I'm thrilled for Jen – and I can't risk telling him about it, not with him knowing Dylan pretty well now. I mean, he'd never say anything intentionally but what if it just slipped out? I lean into Stick's shoulder and bask in feeling so good.

The Goddess Society is working out brilliantly. Despite what Jen thinks, I reckon Jase is perfect for Lia – for a while anyway. And Dylan is perfect for Jen, possibly for ever. And Paul is perfect for me – if only for Saturday night.

8

"Who the *hell* is Pink Wingo?"

I can't really deal with the hugeness of what I'm about to do – confess my feelings to Dylan and put in motion a chain of events that will change my whole life – so I focus on the detail instead. The detail involves trying to tame the frizzy mess that passes for my hair with my mum's tortoiseshell comb and half a bottle of Charles Worthington.

Don't get me wrong, detail doesn't mean trivia – in fact Shelley has a not-so-ancient proverb that goes: get the hair right and everything else will follow.

The doorbell rings, right on time. It's so easy for Dylan to get here now there's the tram right from Croydon to Beckenham Junction. I can hear him downstairs talking to my nan. He loves her, and she loves him back. As well as being naturally charming and a good talker, he's one of the few people we know who remembers my mum, however hazily. I love it that his life crossed over with hers.

Her life. It was like a sparkler, blazing and bright and

then gone. Even her name – Iona – sparkles. I never called her Mummy – I don't know why. Maybe she wanted me to be like one of her friends. She loved the too-thin women that filled our flat with smoke from gold-tipped cigarettes (why I hated them) and poetry (why I forgave them). I still get flashes of her in my mind, frozen into photographs that were never taken. The hem of her charity shop cocktail dress, alive with glittering beads. The smell of her lipstick as she kissed me on her way out for the night. Her long silver-nailed fingers pulling coloured tissues from her handbag, like magician's scarves.

Of course I know it can't all have been sparkles. I know there must have been sulks and smacks and early-to-beds, but I just don't remember them. I don't remember the night she died either, although I was there. The only witness. Lizzy's told me what happened from the minute I knocked on the door of their flat, but that's not the same. And, of course, there's no one to tell me what came before. I don't know why, but I can't help feeling it was my fault, somehow. Apparently that's quite usual when something tragic happens, even if you were nowhere near. You know, people think *if only* this or that. But the difference is that I *was* there. The only witness. And what scares me is that I can't remember anything about it. Sometimes, when I'm doing visualizations, I try to go back there, to find some part of myself I suspect may be stranded in that night, in that cold, lilac bathroom. But I can't. Velvet curtains swish shut over my memory – and though it startles me that there are parts of myself even *I'm* not allowed access to, I'm kind of relieved. I know it's got something to do with the silver sandal of Mum's that I've got on my dressing table, though. It gave me such a start when Shelley kicked hers off the other day. For a minute I felt five years old again. I thought I was going to remember something. But then I clicked back into me, here, now.

It doesn't matter. Like I said, I've got things to remember Mum by, on my dressing table. Her comb, the silver sandal (I don't know why I've only got one – the other must have got lost at some point, I suppose), a few photos and candles and her copy of *Ariel*, with her notes scribbled in the margins. I sometimes see echoes of her in present things too, like Shelley's strappy shoes. Sometimes when she's got a new pair I have to stop myself saying, *wow, Mum'd love those*. Yeah, I call her Mum now. It makes me feel closer to her somehow, as if she belongs only to me. And anyway, she's not around to stop me. There's a shadow of her now in my (finally) sleek, straight black hair as I check the back of it with a hand mirror. For a moment I imagine her standing back to back with me, saying, "Good luck, Jenny-bean. I always liked that boy."

"Jen! It's Dylan!"

I jump, thinking I've conjured her ghost or something, but then I realize it's just Nan calling up the stairs. "One second!" I shout back, breaking the spell of Mum.

When she was alive I knew I didn't have a dad, but I didn't know I had a nan. She came after. Social Services tracked her down. She didn't even know I existed because she and Mum hadn't spoken for years. We came as a surprise to each other – a relief too. There was something left after all.

When I get downstairs, Nan says, "You shouldn't leave me alone with a nice young fella like this. Who knows what we might get up to!"

Dylan plays along. "Too right, Mrs L!"

His laughter sends a hot shiver right through me as I walk into the living room.

"Hi angel," he says, just about waiting for me to sit down before tucking into the plate of bread and butter Nan always puts on the table.

"Hi." I sneak a look at his short dark hair, waxed into a peak at the front, his tanned skin, high cheekbones and, as he catches me looking, wide-mouthed grin.

I've seen him so often I should have stopped being floored by his looks by now. Instead it seems to get worse every time. His short-sleeved Salt Rock shirt has big surfy-style blue flowers printed on it, and while I can't see his legs (shame!) I guess he's wearing his favourite hemp baggies.

The phone rings, but I don't go to answer it. In reply

to Dylan's raised eyebrows I say, "It'll be Lia again. For about the gazillionth time. She's just started seeing this guy, and she keeps phoning up and rerunning their night in the pub. She didn't call me about it for a while, but she's certainly making up for that now. It gets more technicolour every time she tells it."

Nan comes in with two steaming plates of food. "It's even getting a bit dull for me and you know how I love juicy gossip," she says, putting the plates down in front of me and Dylan. Dylan takes a big sniff of the steam, like he's going to go "Ah, Bisto!" Dinner is nut loaf with mushroom gravy for us, which I made earlier, and individual chicken chasseur for Nan. Nan's dinner has been on a long and fascinating journey from farm to factory to freezer to microwave to plate, but that's the way she likes it. I notice that she's even put napkins on the table and the vegetables in a separate bowl – in this house that's really going to town. But then, she always makes an effort for Dylan.

"Dylan was telling me about the CD they're making at school," says Nan.

He grimaces at me as if to say it was more her winkling the information out of him than him going on about it. "It's just the end of term compilation," he says, "and I've been asked to write a song for it. No big deal."

"An *original* song," says Nan proudly, as if he were her own grandson. "Have you got any ideas yet?"

"A few riffs and that," says Dylan, shovelling

another big forkful of dinner into his mouth, "but I'm still finding my own style. My tutors are really helping, but it's something that has to come from me, in the end."

Dylan's on this amazing music course at the Brit School – it covers just about everything from composing, to recording, to the business side. Thank God there's a free place where you can learn that stuff, or people like Dylan might never get to develop their talent. He tells us how they've had a scout from a record company round, looking to put a boy band together. "It's not really my scene, you know?" he says, clearing his plate before we've even made a dent in our dinners and taking Nan's cue to help himself to more. "I mean, I want my contribution to this world to be more than leaping around in front of a load of twelve-year-olds, singing *ooh, baby, baby.*"

"So you didn't go for it?" I say, half-impressed and half-disappointed. My boyfriend the pop star. My husband the pop star.

Dylan shrugs and digs into his seconds. "Sure I did. You've got to think where these things might lead. Just look at Robbie Williams."

"Oh, I'd like to do more than just *look* at Robbie Williams!" says Nan. "Now there's a lovely young man! I wouldn't mind being stuck in a very small elevator with *him*!"

Dylan grins. "Steady on, Mrs L. I don't want you

going mad over another man! I'm relying on you to be my number one fan."

Nan winks at him. "You can count on it, dear. Just don't forget me when you're rich and famous." That's her standard line.

"Couldn't if I tried," says Dylan, finishing his second plateful and sitting back looking highly contented.

Nan grins and says, "Anyone for Vienetta?"

After dessert, Dylan and I help Nan with the washing up, then head up to my room. Dylan looks surprised as he walks through the door. "Wow, Jen, you've really tidied this place up. And that's a new bedspread thingy, isn't it?"

I smile, loving that he notices things like that.

"Been having someone special over, have you? Come on, spill."

"Kind of," I say. I turn to my stereo and fiddle with my CDs to compose myself. I pretend to take time choosing one, though I already decided this morning that it was going to be *Boys for Pele*. I call on Pele, the Hawaiian volcano goddess, to be with me. My legs have gone numb and, God knows, I feel like I need her. This is it, I tell myself.

Carpe diem.

When I turn around again, Dylan's sitting on the edge of the bed. I have a fleeting thought that maybe I won't have to do it. That maybe he's going to say something to *me*. He certainly looks serious enough. I sit down next to him and steel myself. I'm about to say the words when. . .

"Jen, I've got something to tell you."

Me too, I think.

"About feelings and stuff."

Me too, I think.

"I've been meaning to say something for a long time."

Me too, I think.

"It's just, it's been hard to find the words, you know?"

Damn right, I know. It's like he's reading my mind. Well, *that* shouldn't be so surprising. We're meant for each other. Of course we feel absolutely and utterly the same.

That's what gives me the courage to lean forward and ever so gently brush his lips with mine.

Dylan leans forward too and kisses me back. The kiss gets deeper and stronger – like being pulled underwater. It's as if every moment we've ever spent together has been leading to this. When we surface I slowly open my eyes and look up at my best friend, my The One, my soon to be first and only lover.

"I'm gay," says Dylan.

I stare at him. *"What?"*

"I'm gay," he says again. "I was going to say something the other night. I've been desperate to tell someone, but I knew it wasn't the right time. . ."

This is what he was going to tell me? And all the time I thought. . .

My whole past and my whole future rush away into some dark vortex. All that's left is this tiny patch of present here on the purple velvet bedcover. I'm totally confused, like I lost consciousness and woke up in a completely different world. "But why did you kiss me?"

"Because I love you," he says simply. "But . . . oh. . ." He peers at me. "Why did you kiss *me*? You don't. . ."

I force myself to giggle. "Oh, God, no! Don't flatter yourself! It's just this, erm, thing I've got going on with the girls. They bet me a pizza you were a good kisser and I said I bet you weren't, so they said I had to find out, so. . ."

It's the lamest excuse in the history of the universe, but it's the only one I can think of right now. Amazingly he seems to swallow it – lucky he's so wrapped up in his own stuff.

"So, how was I?"

"Excuse me?"

"Well, you know, what are you going to tell the girls?"

That you are the best kisser this side of Brad Pitt. "Oh, yeah, well, that's one free pizza for me, I reckon." I shudder dramatically. "Thank God you're not going to inflict *that* on womankind." Dylan laughs and gives me the fake daggers. I keep smiling, but my mind's going crazy. This doesn't even make sense. "But you've been out with girls before," I say.

"Yeah, I was just trying to fit in, I think, but I can't pretend any more."

I can't believe it. I *won't* believe it. "But just the other night, you said about that barmaid at the studio."

Dylan half-smiles. "Actually, Stick mentioned that. I just went along with it. That's why I want this out in the open. I feel like I'm not really being myself when things like that happen – you know, like I'm not being honest with people."

"But what if it's just a phase?" I say. "Loads of people experiment at our age."

Dylan laughs. "Jen, I'm not trying to be trendy! I've felt this way since before I knew what being gay *was*."

I cringe. Perversely, I understand him completely. I've been in love with him since before I knew what being in love was. "But. . ." I begin.

Dylan gives me an intense look. "Jen, what the hell's going on? You're the last person I expected to be weird about this. I feel like I'm being interrogated here."

I suddenly realize what I'm doing. "Sorry. It's just all a bit . . . out of the blue."

Dylan sighs. "No, look, *I'm* sorry. You're entitled to react however you like. It's just, I really need you right now, you know?"

91

"I know."

"Oh, Jen, I knew you were the right person to tell."

I run my fingers through my hair. My beautiful sleek, smooth hair. How can this be happening? *Get the hair right and everything else will follow.* That's the proverb, isn't it? Dylan doesn't know it, but I was absolutely the *wrong* person to tell.

I lean into him, rigid, heart pounding. I've been waiting so long for this moment. If I just hold on I can pretend that this is still my dream, that we kiss again, and again, and make love, and then get a flat together and that, after lots more practice at the kissing and the sex between lectures at university, we get married and have kids and get a Volvo and. . .

"Jen, what's wrong?" Dylan holds me away and looks right at me. Which is a shame because my dream doesn't include silently crying big black streaks of mascara down my face.

"Wrong? Oh, God, no. Nothing's wrong. It's just, it's a big thing for you and it won't be easy. . ."

Dylan pulls me close again. "Oh, Jen, you sweetheart."

Stop touching me. Stop holding me. No, don't stop. *Just stop being gay*, I think, calling on all my mystical powers of manifestation.

"Jen, I want you to go out with me," says Dylan.

I blink at him. I think I've made something truly

magical happen. "Yuh?" is all I manage to say.

"Yeah. To a club. I want to meet someone. But I'm not up for going on my own and I don't want to tell anyone else yet, you know, people from school and that. Oh, please, Jen. Go on."

"A *gay* club?" I say, sounding like a cross between Mary Whitehouse and the Pope.

He grins shyly. "That's kind of the point."

I stare at him. Outrageous! What a cheek! I mean, *hello*? Spurned goddess dying of unrequited love here! "You want me to come to a gay club and hang out with you till you meet someone then vanish like Pink Wingo?" I take a deep breath and remind myself that he doesn't know I'm suffering from unrequited anything.

"Yeah, that'd be great," says Dylan, my sarcasm sliding right off him. Then he frowns. "Who the *hell* is Pink Wingo?"

I sigh. "It doesn't matter." He's obviously forgotten all about Pink Wingo and Lady Fabula the pop-star-princess-witches. Well, at least this explains why we always fought over the tiara.

"So you'll come?"

Something in Dylan's voice tells me just how much this means to him. "Course I will," I say, giving up on seething fury and settling for gracious resignation instead.

"Oh God, thanks, Jen," says Dylan, hugging me again. "I love you."

I hug him back fiercely, like he's just been rescued from a burning building. "I love you too," I whisper.

Then he goes out to the corner shop, for a *Time Out*. I stand in the kitchen waiting for the kettle to boil. I'm going to deal with it, honest. I'm really going to stick with the whole gracious resignation thing. And I'm *never* going to let him know how I feel. Thank God he spoke first. One second more and he would have found out. I'm honestly vowing to be there for him and love him as my oldest friend. But every time I close my eyes he's kissing me and I'm under that ocean, lost in a complete bliss which. . .

. . .which won't ever happen again.

And when I think that, I'm furious – not with Dylan, but with myself.

I curse my stars, my palm, my tarot, my tea leaves and my downright stupidity. I must need some sort of emotional glasses. Honestly! What an idiot. I mean, here's this guy who's funny, sensitive, has great dress sense and eats nut loaf. HELLO? OF COURSE HE'S GAY, YOU STUPID GIRL!

You're in the wrong queue. Your blokes are the fat mumbly ones over there in the corner of the pub. Yes, that's right, they're the ones who wear enough Lynx to choke a horse and only watch *Friends* in case Jennifer Aniston ever wears that boob-popping dress again. You know, the ones who think good foreplay means getting your bra undone without taking their eyes off *Top Gear*.

I start having this imaginary conversation with Dylan that goes:

Me: I know you think you're gay but you're just confused. What you need is a good woman to set you straight (I even do imaginary puns – how sad!), hey, for example how about *me*?

Dylan: Oh, yeah, you're so right. Thanks, Jen. I love you, please be my soul mate and stay with me for ever. . . Oh, and also? I really think we should get a Volvo.

And then Dylan kisses me again and fireworks explode over the bay where we're standing by the water's edge (I'm a romantic, so shoot me!) and then we're tossing aside our empty champagne glasses and tumbling on to the deserted moonlit beach and it's like, *Alert! Alert! Beautiful goddess about to lose virginity in non-tacky way with non-gay love of life!* And that's where I come to and it all explodes, because Dylan is gay, and there's nothing I can do about it.

Or is there?

As the kettle boils this crazy kamikaze voice bubbles up from the back of my head and says, *Don't give up yet, Jen. Dylan may not realize it but this is just a phase.* It sounds remarkably like something Shelley would say.

So Dylan gets back and we have the tea and the

packets of chocolate buttons he's bought. He reads from the club listings and the only way I can get through it is by making myself into a marionette and then pulling my own strings, giving myself stage directions – *smile now, nod now, laugh now*. I hear my own comments as if from far away, sounding strange and alien, jangling in the air.

But Dylan's so nervous and excited he doesn't notice. As far as he's concerned, I'm keen and encouraging and we eventually settle on something called Jinx at Bardot's in Soho this Saturday night. He finishes his tea and we go downstairs. He says goodnight to me and Nan with the same big hug and kiss on both cheeks and I see him to the door. He hugs me again and whispers, "Thanks, Jen. This means so much to me."

Me too, I think, holding him close. And I don't mean the night out.

I go upstairs, sit stiffly on the end of the bed and plan my strategy. God, I really do sound like Shelley now. But there's a good reason for that: Shelley always means business. And as far as Dylan goes, so do I. I feel sick that I've told the girls I'm in love with Dylan – still, I won't tell them what's happened, not just yet. It's not lying as such. It's just that, if my plan works out, I won't have to tell them at all.

You see, it ain't over till the gay boy turns straight.

I pull my goddess books down off my shelf and

spread them over the bed for inspiration. Diana, Roman goddess of hunting. Hather, Egyptian goddess of sensual power. Cerridwen, Celtic goddess of magic loss and renewal. Frigg, Nordic goddess of physical love and wisdom. Amaterasu, Japanese goddess of the sun. Aphrodite and Athene, Greek goddesses of love and war. I call on them all.

Love and war. Aphrodite had a magic girdle, which made her irresistible to men. Athene had a spear and shield to fight her battles. I'll have a vintage long black silk dress and some strappy heels borrowed from Shelley. The kind Mum would have loved. And my Goddess-Society-Approved Underwear, of course – hidden under my armour, like a silky magic spell.

9

"Yeah, right, like my mum's gonna write me a note for *that*."

On Saturday afternoon, the girls come round to mine to swap make-up and clothes and stuff. It's a big day for the Goddess Society. Shel's fixed her date with Paul for tonight, and I've got plans of my own. Shel also told me about Jen and Dylan. I'm dying to know if she's told him how she feels yet, but for once I'm keeping my mouth shut. You want to know the quick way to clam Jen up? Start firing personal questions.

Mum and Dad and Sam have gone to Dorset for the weekend, to this caravan we've got near the beach. SADLY I couldn't go, much as I wanted to, as I've got WAY too much revision to do for my all-important GCSEs, don't you know. Mum and Dad agreed that it would be IMPOSSIBLE to work in a tiny little caravan with Sam's sandy little friends wandering in and out all the time wanting flat warm Coke from the bottle that's too big to fit in the weeny fridge. It's a sacrifice, I know, but one I'm prepared to make for the sake of my education. Damn shame.

Just so I don't go *straight* to hell when I die, I did a bit of reading through my notes in bed this morning, when the ads came on in the middle of the *Friends* reruns. And I do (solemnly) swear I'll do a proper session tomorrow afternoon. But I don't want to overdo it. You hear all these warnings about taking regular breaks from study and not getting too stressed out and throwing yourself off a bridge. So really I sort of *deserve* to have Jase round for a posh dinner tonight, don't I? Actually, I'm planning to have him for breakfast, too.

When we met up in Café Rouge on Thursday lunchtime I took the plunge and asked him over (I didn't have to worry about being caught out of school – everyone knows that's what lunch passes are really *for*). The conversation went something like:

Jase: Oh, by the way, my mum's out at some animal rights conference tomorrow. How about you bunk off and come over to mine? We can get some DVDs, chill out.

Me: Yeah, right, like my mum's gonna write me a note for *that*. "Dear Miss Browne, please excuse my daughter from school today as she has to go round Jason Raines's house and have lots of sex. Yours sincerely, Mrs Isabelle Harcourt. PS Please put me down to provide a fruit cake for the PTA raffle."

Jase: Yuwat?

That's when I realized that he hadn't actually mentioned doing it at all. I was just reacting to the giant thought-stereo on his head, which was blaring, *Hey, come on over and we'll have sex!*

Me: (Unable to speak due to TMS – Total Mortification Syndrome.)

Jase: Well, I didn't mean *just* that. I really like you, Li. (Shrugs.) I just thought . . . but no big deal. . .

Me: How about dinner at mine on Saturday night? The paries are away in Daaarsut. We'll have the house to ourselves. I'll cook something nice.

Jase: (Smiles. Winks. Does one-move fag-lighting thing that melts my insides.) Yeah, OK. Cool.

This is what I'm telling the girls as we lie back on my bed with waxing strips on our legs. Saturday night. It seemed a lifetime away when I invited him. Thursday and Friday felt like a year each, but now Saturday's here and suddenly it's all looming up ahead, like Las Vegas on the desert horizon.

"I think I should be here when he comes over," says Jen suddenly.

I can't help snorting with laughter. "What, so you can hold my hand? I think I can manage to seduce Jase on my own, thanks, mate."

Jen looks scandalized. "I don't mean that! But, well, it's not as if you really know him or anything."

"Oh, listen, it's Stuck Record G-G-Girl," I say. "What,

you think I need a chaperone, like at some high school dance in the 50s?"

Jen glances at Shel for back-up, but Shel just gives her an intense look, like *shut up now*.

But Jen doesn't shut up. It's like she's on some kind of single-handed mission to destroy our friendship. "No. It's just, you're going to have him round here for the night and anything could happen. . ."

"That's what I'm hoping," I say, being deliberately wicked just to wind her up. I can almost see a spring in her head tightening.

"For God's sake, Lia – wake up!" she snaps, sitting bolt upright, suddenly taking the bait. "Not everything in this world always comes out the way you want it. You could be disappointed . . . or get hurt. What if he—"

"What, nicks the silver?" I hiss, not seeing the funny side any more. "Or are you saying he's a rapist or something? For Christ's sake, Jen, chill out, will you?"

"You should both chill out," says Shel.

"She started it!" I shriek. "Ms Doom and Bloody Gloom. I thought negativity was against your religion, Jen. Whatever happened to live and let live?"

"Leave it, Lia," says Shel.

"It's not just me!" Jen shouts. "The cards say Jase is bad news!" She looks shocked that she's come right out with that, but ploughs on. "They aren't often wrong. I did it loads of times and he always came out as a no-go zone!"

"Jen, hang on a—" says Shel.

"Shel swore you were going to back off, but you're worse than ever!" I shout back. "You don't really care about me or you wouldn't be trying to spoil it! I mean, *tarot cards*? I'm not having a load of rubbish like that ruin my first time!"

"*Rubbish?*" yells Jen. "Is that what you think this stuff is? You obviously don't give a damn about *me* if you think my beliefs are *rubbish*!"

"OOOOOOOWWWWWWWW!!!!!!!!" We both scream as Shelley yanks a waxing strip off each of our legs.

"Right, glad I've got your attention," she says crossly. "Jen's not trying to spoil it, Li."

"Could have fooled me," I grump. Shel grabs the edge of another waxing strip and I shut up pretty pronto.

"I just care about you," says Jen.

"Yeah, I know," I say, softening. "But can't you do it in a useful way, like helping me work out what to bloody well cook?"

"Course we will," says Shel. "You know what they say, the way to a man's heart is through his stomach."

"Yeah, but what's the way to his willy?" I ask, and we double up with laughter – even Jen.

102

The girls are brill. We settle on wild mushroom risotto from *The Naked Chef* and this thing in Nigella's book called chocolate cloud cake that's basically this lush chocolate cake thing with cream piled up in the centre. I picked it 'cause it's actually *supposed* to sink in the middle, so there's less chance of it going wrong. When I'm copying down what ingredients I need, I put strawberries as well, thinking I can dot them artistically round on the top. Then we have a bit of a cheese debate. To brie or not to brie? Ha ha. We decide not to 'cause I don't have endless cash.

We've just settled it that instead of a complicated starter I'll get some prawns out of the freezer and pour a bit of seafood sauce over them, when Jen goes, "I'm out with Dylan tonight. . ."

Ha! I knew something was up! Softly, softly catchy monkey.

"Oh. My. God. You told him," goes Shel, eyes ablaze with the possibility of hearing some grade A gossip. "Come on, spill. We have to know *all* the details."

But Jen just looks mysterious. She likes to keep stuff private. Weird or what? Shel looks like she's going to implode with the not knowing, so Jen takes pity on her and gives her a tiny crumb of info. "We're going clubbing." And that's it. That's all we're getting.

I put on my most serious face. "I really think I should be there too, Jen. You've only known him, what, ten years? Anything could happen."

"Ha ha, very funny!" says Jen. Then she changes the subject so fast it's like – swish – dropping the blade of a guillotine. "What I was going to say was, I'll give you his mobile number, then if you do have any kind of trouble. . ."

I open my mouth to really tell her where to go this time but she holds her hands up. "I mean, you know, like if the sinking cake rises or you can't get your eyeliner on straight, you can call me, OK, and I'll come on over."

"All right already!" I do a cross face, but inside I'm quite relieved. Course I don't think Jase is dodgy or anything, but it's nice to have a safety net.

"Is the third goddess's membership expiring tonight too?" asks Shel, trying to reopen the far more interesting subject of Jen and Dylan.

Jen just smiles, like she's completely above this sort of discussion.

"Ooohh, see that look, Shel?" I say. "That means definitely YES! Whoopee – we're all losing it on the same night! How fantastic!"

Jen just narrows her eyes at me but she looks really glowing. "Well, we'll see how things go. All I'm saying is that I've packed Nan off to stay with Great Auntie Rita in Brighton for a fortnight."

"A fortnight! I *knew* there were sparks there – I just knew it, even before Shel told me!" I yell, thrilled. "What's been going on, Jen, hey? What did you say?

What did he say? Did you snog? Have you—"

"Oh yeah, Shel," says Jen, cool as a cucumber, completely ignoring me. "I meant to ask – can I borrow your Valentinos? They'd look really good with my black silk dress."

I know that's truly the end of that, now. I wonder for a second what it would be like to be such a complex person with loads of secrets and a big poetic storm going on under the surface – and I decide I'd way rather be me, big mouth and all, telling everything the second it happens, like BBC News 24.

"OK," says Shel, "you're in luck. I'm probably wearing my silver strappies anyway."

"Thanks, you are *sooooo* the shoe fairy," says Jen.

"I've already bagged the FMBs, haven't I?"

"Yeah, I left them in the hall for you."

"Cheers, Shel."

"FMBs?" Jen repeats, puzzled.

"Fuck Me Boots," I explain. "I'll probably get varicose veins or something in them but who cares? I can always unzip them under the table."

Jen smiles and shakes her head and then scribbles down Dylan's mobile number on the inside cover of *The Naked Chef*. "Anyway, the point is, Li, you can call me, if you want," she says.

"You can call me too," says Shel.

"Oh, Shel, you sweetie," I say. "I know you don't mean it, though."

"Damn right I don't mean it!" she giggles. "I'll probably have it switched to message."

"Oh, far be it for me to interrupt your posh nosh at, where is it again?"

"Palm Court Brasserie, actually. Little French place in Covent Garden. I've got it all worked out. Oysters. Champagne. Some big juicy roast thing with braised baby shallots and about three bits of asparagus draped over the top. Then back to Paul's flat for dessert."

Shelley rummages in the purple bag next to her and pulls out a silver box just smaller than a shoebox. I think she's got a cake in it or something, you know, for dessert, until I see that on the top it says, in purple glitter pen, "Box of Tricks". I am a total der-brain sometimes. "Oh. *Dessert*."

Jen's bracing herself, like she's scared the Box of Tricks is going to be full of pervy stuff like handcuffs and all that. How cool would that be? But when Shel opens the lid it's just pretty things in little beds of pink tissue paper.

"Massage oil, scented candles, incense sticks, the ultimate sexy mix CD, chocolate body paint," says Shelley, tapping her newly manicured nails on the jar. "Oh, and condoms, obviously."

I make a mental note to get candles and that when I go out for the food. What was I planning to do? Lose my virginity in complete darkness or under a

100-watt bulb? I suddenly feel a wave of panic rise up from my feet and break in my chest. Jase is coming over in less than four hours and I haven't organized *anything*.

When we say goodbye it's a bit more meaningful than usual.

"Just think," says Shel, "when we next see each other, we might not be virgins any more."

We do the kind of squealy huggy dancy thing that you normally only see on American TV. It's really girly but for some reason it feels right today. We're making our own history here. We're making memories for when we're old and wrinkly. It's a squealy huggy dancy sort of thing.

The girls head off so that Jen can get the shoes from Shel's and I walk the other way, up to the supermarket. I didn't know there *were* so many sorts of mushrooms – chanterelles, blewits, girolles, oysters, shitake, chestnuts, field – let alone that you can stick them all in the same recipe if you want.

Next I have to get celery. Not very difficult, you're thinking, for a girl taking eight GCSEs, but it starts this major whirligig in my head. Do you have to buy a whole bunch (?) bulb (?) just to get one stick? Are you allowed to break some off, like you can with grapes? I'm not sure about that, so I don't, just in case. Then I go through a phase of nearly deciding not to bother at all, but then I think the celery might be the vital part of the dish or something but if that's true and the whole thing is going to just taste of celery anyway then why make it at all because, like, *yuck*, but I haven't got the ingredients written down for anything else and the only thing I know off by heart is shepherd's pie and well, that's not exactly cool, is it? That's when I realize my thoughts are just going round and round like a sort of mad maypole dance, and now my brain's all knotted up. I've been standing in the same spot with my hand hovering over the damn celery for so long that the bloke unpacking the red peppers probably thinks I'm trying to heal its aura or something. Huh. Maybe I'm not as cool with all this dinner stuff as I thought.

When I get round the store to the drinks section I spend ages dithering over which bottle of wine to get. I reckon there's less chance of being asked my age if I get it in here in a trolley with a load of other stuff, like it's just part of my normal life, instead of going specially to Oddbins. Eventually I go for a Valpolicella, 'cause that's what Shel always orders when we go for a pizza.

As the guy beeps the wine through the check-out I get this paranoia that an alarm'll go off and a blue light'll shine on me and it'll be like – *Alert! Alert! Small child trying to buy alcohol!* I wish I had a credit card instead of cash – even a debit card – I reckon that makes you look older. But there are no flashing lights or sirens and so I go home and have the most nightmarish two hours of my life freaking out about whether the risotto rice I've got will still work, even though it's different from the kind Jamie recommends in the book, and whether the egg whites are ever going to turn into fluffy peaks like they're supposed to (then when they do I spend ages staring into the bowl wondering how the hell they actually *do* that). Then I realize I'm being a loon again, like over the celery, and so I remind myself that there are actually people starving to death in other countries, so it's really bad of me to worry about stupid stuff like the bloody egg whites.

The cake comes out OK (so it should, I sat on the kitchen floor and supervised it through the oven door) and I get all the stuff ready in little bowls for the risotto. I set the table, adding some of the little tea-light candles I bought at Waitrose, and put the prawn cocktails in the fridge. Then I go upstairs, have a long shower, spend ages trying to get the set leg wax off my duvet cover, then give up and put a fresh one on out of the airing cupboard.

When it comes to it, I've only got about fifteen minutes to get dressed and do my hair and make-up. Shit! I try on Shelley's boots with the purple suede mini-skirt and black shirt I bought with Nana's birthday money. It looks brill, but the boots pinch my toes and they're so tight up the leg I can hardly walk down the stairs, so I take them off and stand them by the door, ready to put on just before Jase arrives.

Then I pour myself a glass of wine, find Mum's least

disgusting pinny and start the risotto. I want to be halfway through it when Jase gets here, so the house is filled with beautiful smells. I want to open the door with my wine glass in one hand and a wooden spoon in the other so he thinks I'm not only a sex kitten but a domestic goddess as well. I suddenly remember about music and have to sprint to put some on, because I'm not sure how long you can not stir the risotto for without it going claggy (I'm supposed to be giving it my loving and undivided attention for about seventeen minutes, according to Jamie). Pink blares through the house, doing "Just Like a Pill", and I get into singing along and stirring the risotto.

When the doorbell rings I dash to answer it, and have to stay bent down low 'cause I don't want Jase to see my bizarre wine-wooden-spoon-boots-juggling monkey impression through the glass panel. Eventually I get it all sorted and answer the door.

This is it. Showtime.

110

10

"I'm off to devil-worshipping class, if you must know."

Jen leaves with the shoes, but without saying a single word more about Dylan (even though I told her I have a rare disease which means if I don't hear at least ten minutes worth of fresh, juicy gossip per day my brain explodes).

I put on an Ibiza chill-out-mix CD and start thinking about what to wear. I try on a few things and in the end I go for these low cut hipster jeans that are really tight round the bum and thighs but flared at the bottom, with pre-faded bits on so you look like you've spent the last three years on a horse ranch. I decide to go a bit further down the country rock chick road with my red boots and vintage black leather coat. I lay the stuff out on my bed, along with the Goddess-Society-Approved Underwear and make for the shower.

I can't find any hair bands (where do they go? I swear I buy ten a week) so I grab a pair of black Marks' knicks from my drawer and tie my hair up with those. I should go on one of those "survive on a desert island" programmes, shouldn't I? I'd be pole fishing and making my bra into a pair of shoes in no time. I spend ages in the shower getting thoroughly de-fuzzed and exfoliated, using all my nice Molton Brown goodies, then further ages in my purple silk kimono dressing gown from Toast touching up my toenail varnish and polishing the boots.

I'm glad I sorted the Box of Tricks out earlier. Jen's face! I swear she thought there was something pervy in it. It's not that I wouldn't be into that sort of stuff. It's just I want my first time to be simple, kind of *textbook*. I'm staging it a bit tonight, with the clothes and the Box, but it's fun, like I'm getting ready to act in a movie that I'm directing and producing and everything. I'm even the star. Well, the co-star. With Paul.

Mmm, lights, camera, action.

The clock's ticking on up to six and I know I'd better move if I'm going to be fashionably but not rudely late to the Zed Bar where we're meeting for a drink before dinner. I pull the jeans on, and a grey chiffon top with little silver stars on that you can see my purple lacy Goddess-Society-Approved bra through. It's one of those lovely push-up ones that makes the most of what you've got, even if what you've got's not much.

I do my make-up in the dressing-table mirror, pretty natural with just a bit more soft black kohl around the eyes than usual. When I look up I see Mum standing in the doorway, a cigarette dripping from her fingers. "Can you *not* smoke in my flat," I say.

"I'm not *in* your flat," she points out, wiggling her painted toenails to show she hasn't crossed the border where the carpet changes colour from her brown shag pile to my purple with silver weave.

"Your cigarette is." God, sometimes she's more like an annoying younger sister than a mother.

She raises her eyebrows as if to say, *stroppy teenagers, what do you do with them?* and sucks pointedly on the end of the fag. "Dan says he's going to leave his wife for me," she announces. "Lord, I hope not. The whole *point* is that he's already committed. I've told him, forget it. I'm not ironing his bloody shirts."

I do my best to ignore this. I don't want to get involved. I've been listening to this crap ever since I was a little kid, wide-eyed over my chocolate milk.

"Well, aren't you going to say anything?"

I shrug. "If you want the Oprah treatment, call a coven meeting." My mum's got this group of hideous friends who are all pink nails, B&H and hairspray. All they talk about is men.

She gives me an evil look and shuffles off. "Where are you going, then?" she calls from her living room.

"I'm off to devil-worshipping class, if you must know," I say acidly. "Then there's a mass orgy at my favourite dope den."

"Have a nice time, then," she calls, without a hint of

113

sarcasm. I hear her flipping the pages of a magazine. Probably *Vogue* or *W*. I knew she wasn't listening anyway.

I pull on my leather coat and shove my mobile in my bag with my purse, my little kit of make-up re-touching stuff, toothbrush, spare knicks, chewing gum and the Box of Tricks. Then I hitch the bag on to my shoulder and lean in close to the mirror to do a last make-up check. "Actually, *Mother*, I won't be back tonight," I watch myself say. "I'm losing it – in style. So, when you next see me, I won't be a virgin any more."

I pick up my bag and turn around. She's standing right there in the doorway. I have a fleeting hope there's been a freak nicotine side effect and she's gone stone deaf but. . . "You're still a *virgin*?"

"Yeah, so?" I look straight at her, hand on my jutting hip. Her surprise pisses me off. But then, I guess it makes sense. She probably thinks I lost it ages ago with some photographer or stylist or something. Maybe she'd assumed that's how I got into modelling in the first place. A mean little voice in the back of my head says, *well, that's how* she *did*.

I fuss with my lipgloss, watching her in the mirror. I see her smile self-consciously. "Well, enjoy it, then," she says, "and be careful, won't you?"

We catch eyes and both giggle awkwardly, amused at her saying such a mothery-type thing. For a minute I think she's going to hug me, which would be just *squirm*, because we gave up on the mother/ daughter bonding thing when they cut the umbilical cord. Luckily she seems to change her mind and stretches her arms upwards. Phew. I don't want her to ruin my make-up.

I get into the Zed Bar at about eight minutes past seven, the perfect lateness, and spot Paul straight away. He looks amazing in black Paul Smith cords and a petrol-coloured shirt that has this oil rainbow effect when he moves. He's already got a bottle of Grolsch in his hand. When he sees me he strides over and pulls me close to kiss both cheeks. This group of blonde secretary-type girls all start staring at me and whispering – they must have been staking him out. I want to give them the Vs while pretending to scratch my nose, but it's not the sort of thing you do on your perfect date, so I just ignore them.

"You look great," says Paul.

"Thanks," I say. *So do you*, I think, but I don't mention it. I want to play it cool. And anyway, his head's probably big enough as it is.

"Drink?"

"Glass of house white, please."

Paul gets another beer, and my wine, and we find a table in the back room.

"So, how did you get here?" he asks.

"Drove. I've got an MGB, a recon job."

Paul's still silent, looking at me, so I reach for

something else to say about it. "I just got Classic Car mag and picked one out. I'm not that into the mechanics of things, but I like the retro look. . ." I tail off pathetically.

Luckily he speaks then, 'cause that's everything I know about cars used up. "Yeah, I like those, but I'd rather have something modern. I got my TT from Whetstone Audi, with a guarantee and all that. You know where you are then, if something goes wrong." Paul pauses to take a big slug of his beer. God, he's got beautiful hands. Strong and tanned and gleaming with a couple of really tasteful chunky silver rings. "Did you have trouble finding a parking space round here?"

"I parked at my agency," I tell him. "They've got a couple of allocated spaces that are free for us to use in the evenings if we want." I bite the inside of my cheeks to stop myself from laughing. I sound soooooo dull, but Paul seems interested enough.

"Cool. That's a great perk, isn't it? I took the tube. It's only a few stops to get here. I get one resident's permit and one visitor's so it's easier to leave the car at home. It's a good scheme, the parking thing. Stops commuters clogging up our street. You have to pay for the badges at the start of every year. It's only about 100 quid. That's for each one, not for both," he adds, as if it's a vitally important bit of information I can't live without.

"Not bad," I say, just about keeping a straight face.

"Only two hundred for the two. And it must be useful when your family and friends come over. It's hell trying to park in London."

"Yeah, so you're really lucky with that free space at the agency." Paul smiles at me then slugs back some more beer.

Oh. My. God. I'm on my dream date and we're talking about parking. *Parking*.

"So, where do you live?" I say, trying to change the subject.

"Holland Park."

"Holland *Park*," I repeat, taking a sip of wine to avoid laughing. "Very nice."

"Yeah. It's lovely round there. You'll have to come over one day when it's nice weather and we'll have a picnic or something."

"Yeah, I'd like that," I say, grinning. "I could road-test your visitor's permit."

Paul looks at me like he's trying to tell whether I'm taking the piss. I blink at him sweetly as if I'm utterly not. God, why am I such a total *bitch*? Why can't I just be nice and normal instead of finding everything deeply amusing? Small talk is *supposed* to be inane and boring. That's why it's called small talk. *He* knows it's just an act, an ice-breaker. Shit, I hope he does, anyway.

Seeing as I'm obviously crap at the conversation side of things, I try the physical. I pull his hand towards me, run my fingers over the two silver rings and get a total thunderbolt of lust through my body. By his face I can tell he's getting it too. Just from that tiny touch. Jeez, imagine what it'll be like when. . . "These are gorgeous."

"*You're* gorgeous."

Paul knows he's just melted my ice-cream, and we're back on solid ground. He glances at his watch. "We'd better get going. Reservations were for half seven." He stands up and helps me on with my jacket. We hold hands all the way through the pub (I wink at the secretary blondes on my way out) and all the way down the street to the restaurant.

The starter goes really well. I pick the chargrilled asparagus and Paul has the lobster and basil risotto. We sink most of a bottle of wine with it.

"You ought to ease up, Shel," says Paul, "you're driving home, aren't you?"

"Maybe. But I want to enjoy myself. I can always cab it back and pick up my car in the morning."

"Whatever you think."

What I think is that I'll be seeing your flat a lot sooner than Picnic Day, mate. By the small smile on his face I know he knows that too. That I'm drinking just enough so I can't drive back. That this cab home stuff is a load of BS. I can't help wondering how many times he's had this conversation before. Possibly in this actual restaurant. Possibly at this actual table.

I wonder if he knows it's the first time I've done this.

Well, if he doesn't I'm not telling him. That's going to be my secret. However many times he's been here before, that gives me the upper hand. I signal to the waiter for another bottle of wine and we chat about designers and photographers and high street stores and who we like working for and who we don't.

We're almost silent over a main course of pan roast fillet of beef, apart from a few stray comments about the food and the place, because it's just so tasty. It even looks pretty much how it did in my imagination (minus the asparagus, plus some wild mushrooms, ravioli and truffle jus). I've realized that small talk *is* Paul's talk, but I'm telling myself, *so what?* I didn't pick him for his witty conversation. I'll say one thing for him, though. He knows how to dish out the compliments.

"You looked great in that Lipsy campaign," he says, putting his knife and fork together and draping his napkin on the table. "That style really suited you. The guy they put you with looked like a wanker, though."

"Tom? I thought he looked pretty cool actually. I loved the way Flora got his hair sticking right up, even though it's quite long. And that thing Jerome did with his sunglasses and the oversized chain was wicked."

Paul goes silent, twisting one of the gorgeous silver rings round and round. Then he virtually grunts, "It was OK, I guess. Course, it's already been done a million times, but whatever."

"Yeah, on boots and stuff," I argue, "but not on

sunglasses. And Tom's got that lovely fine-featured impish face, so it just looked even sexier."

Paul reaches into his pocket and pulls out Marlboro Lights and a lighter with black suede on it. He takes one and lights it without offering me the pack. He smokes intensely, like there are now three people at the table – him, me and the cigarette. He's clearly finding the cigarette better company.

I *have* to get it back on track. I want to just say, "Have I offended you?" like I would with Stick or the girls, but I know that's not the done thing outside mates. I realize Paul wasn't talking about the *Lipsy* campaign shoot at all. He was talking about how any other blokes that come near me are tossers. Am I supposed to find that attractive? I mean, why not just pee up my leg or something, if he's that territorial? We're only on one date. Jeez, what's he going to be like after we've slept together? I remind myself that I won't really care what he's like then, and relax a bit. I have to bring him round if I want things to work out as planned. It's sad, but I have to play the game.

"About that shoot," I say carefully. "Tom looked good, sure, but he was pretty dull to hang around with all day. Lucky I remembered my book."

Paul instantly cheers up. It's too easy. Like giving a kid a chocolate bar. I feel bad for betraying Tom, who's perfectly sweet. Over the flickering candle on our table, and on my fourth glass of wine, Paul should look even

120

more sexy than ever. But for some reason he looks less. I can't shake the image out of my mind of a pouting little boy.

This time Paul offers me a cigarette before he lights up. I don't take one but I take his hand over the table instead. There's still a big zing, but not like before. I try to just look at his face, to just see the beautiful almond eyes and stubbly chin and high cheekbones. For a minute it works and I'm in zing city. Our eyes lock and he's just leaning across the table and. . .

"I'd better just check my messages," I say suddenly. "My friend Lia's got this really important thing on and she might have called."

"Sure." Gravelly flippant voice, through the cigarette between his lips. Like James Dean. Was that sultry or just plain sulky?

I pull out my mobile, flip the lid and beep around for a minute while I try to think. Why did I put off kissing him?

Paul nips to the loo, thank God. I actually have a message, but not from Lia. It's Stick, with this running joke we've got about a completely unexpected donkey. It makes me crease up and snort with laughter.

The wine's obviously loosened up my mind and I think about Stick and the maybe kiss, and how he took my hand under the table and how that made me feel. Course, at the time I put it down to mad hormones or the vibrating mobile, but what if it was something else?

Something more? I get flooded with good vibes then and hit the recall button, just to see his name come up on the screen.

The problem is, open yourself to good feelings and you automatically open yourself to bad. Suddenly I think about Stick going to the Nines' gig with *someone* and I get a sharp pang in my chest, exactly the same as when he told me. Is it really just my ego-thingy?

Or is it my heart?

I imagine Stick out with Little Miss Broody Suicide, whoever she is – getting her a drink, holding her hand in the street, telling her she looks gorgeous – and I feel sick. Then I start wondering – would Stick care if he knew I was out with someone else, doing all the above?

What the hell am I thinking? Stick *said* I wasn't his type. So that's the end of that.

Paul sits back down and I push thoughts of Stick aside. This is what I decided to do and this is what I'm doing. It'll be all right when we get to the sex. That'll make up for a not-great date.

"Any messages?"

"Nothing important," I say, "just some joke about a donkey."

Paul lights up again and just sits looking at me, smoking. I suddenly realize that he's waiting for me to tell him the joke. But I know he wouldn't get it.

I shrug. "Stick's got a weird sense of humour." I

don't mention that I have too, and that laughing at the joke is the best thing that's happened so far this evening.

"Stick. Funny name. He your brother or something?"

"Something like that."

I try to focus on here and now and Paul, but my stupid wine-soaked mind won't let me. If I'm spending what's meant to be my perfect date with Paul thinking about someone else, then will I really be able to focus on him later? Do I really want to share my first time with him? At the moment I don't even want to share a joke with him.

Not Stick's joke.

Suddenly, it feels like I'm betraying Stick by just sitting here. It's like I hadn't noticed that we're actually having this meal on a train track, and BOOM! I've just been hit by the Number 45 Realization Express.

I think I want to be with Stick.

True, he's not my type, but there's something there that I can't explain. And as for him being with someone else, well, I'm used to getting what I want, so I'll just have to change his mind about her, won't I? I was here before she came along, and I'll damn well be here after she's gone.

I have my methods. Hmm, I certainly do. Have you ever raised your eyebrows at your own thoughts?

So, when the waiter comes round with the sweet

menus I accept one. As I pretend to dither over dessert, I hatch a new plan. It's probably crazy, and there's a good chance it won't work, but I have to take the risk. They say there's a thin line between insanity and genius – and I reckon I'm walking on it.

I order the strawberry soufflé and then sit back and really listen to Paul telling me about his recent shoot in LA for *Popsicle*.

I'm all ears, all *his*. For now, anyway.

11

"Make them doubles and forget the Coke."

Dylan calls round for me at about half nine. We were planning to meet at Victoria, but he said he'd be over this way organizing a Music Club event at the Studio anyway. I open the door and he does this looking me up and down really slowly thing and wolf-whistling. "You look stunning," he says.

Well, I wanted to make an effort for you, I think. "Well, I wanted to make an effort for your big night," I say.

"Your nan not about?"

"No, she had to go to Brighton." I can't help smiling to myself when I say that. "Do you want to come in for a drink first, or. . ."

"Nah. Let's just get going, shall we?"

We walk up to the train station, linking arms. This is good news because Shelley's shoes are a size too big on me so I have to scrunch my toes up to keep them on. Also, one of the heels seems to be coming loose. We pass lots of couples looking at the menus outside restaurants and walking down to the pubs. I love the fact that we're part of that too. That anyone would think we were together, and that maybe we lived in one of the converted Victorian flats just off the high street.

We don't talk much on the train, instead we just stare out of the window and smile at each other occasionally. Dylan seems really nervous and when we go through the tunnel at Sydenham Hill he spends ages fiddling with his hair in the blacked-out window glass. The silence is fine with me. I don't want to spoil my fantasy with any discussion about the whole stupid gay thing. In my head we're renting a flat at the moment but hoping to buy in the next couple of years when we've saved enough for the deposit, when Dylan's band gets off the ground (and by the way we also have a cat called Sparkle).

We're going to take the tube to Soho but I say, "Let's walk," and slip my hand into his. We go up past the Houses of Parliament, looking at Big Ben and Westminster Abbey. I love walking through the city at night. I love the clink of my heels on the pavement and the way we squeeze a little closer together to let people go by. We go up Whitehall past the Cenotaph and right by the gates of Downing Street. Then we're into Trafalgar Square, walking between the fountains and the National Gallery, where we sometimes come on a Sunday afternoon. We go past Cecil Court where I spend hours in Watkins, my favourite bookshop, which specializes in mysticism and the occult.

As we turn into Romilly Street I suggest stopping at Pete's for a coffee or a quick snack. Pete's is this all-night cafe and deli. Sometimes there's someone set up in the corner doing a bit of acoustic folk rock. I imagine us cocooned on one of the sofas, sipping lattes, talking about poetry, forgetting to go to the bloody club altogether. For some reason I see this in black and white, like we're in some old movie where the heroines were glam and even if the leading men were gay they at least had the decency to *pretend* they weren't.

"Do you mind if we skip Pete's tonight, Jen?" says Dylan. "I might bottle it if we don't just. . ."

"Yeah, sure, whatever you want."

So I pretend not to mind and we keep walking, cutting down Moor Street to get to Old Compton Street. It's still early so there's not much of a queue outside Bardot's and we virtually go right in. Dylan pays for us both. We give our coats in at the cloakroom and wander inside. That's when my stomach sinks right down into my borrowed Valentinos.

I don't know what I'd expected. A bunch of awkward blokes grooving half-heartedly to YMCA, maybe?

But no. They're gorgeous. All of them. So this is where all those great guys you clock in the street hang out. I almost feel relief: *This* is why they don't clock me back, not my small left eye or my big nose. But the relief soon turns to panic. It's just me against this huge clump of beautiful men, all with perfect rhythm, brimming self-confidence and well-shaped eyebrows. Suddenly my slinky black number doesn't feel so special any more. It's crazy – I mean, how can people in jeans and various tight T-shirts make you feel underdressed? But they do. It's as if they had glamour injected into their genes before birth. Dylan hovers beside me. He seems a bit intimidated too. As long as I can keep him away from that dance floor, I'm still in with a chance.

We weave our way towards the bar. Dylan leans across and orders. "Two Bacardi and Cokes please." He looks back towards the dance floor again and quails, adding, "Make them doubles, and forget the Coke." Usually I'd just have the Coke – but I need the Dutch courage as much as he does. We hover around sipping the drinks and watching the dance floor, occasionally smiling nervously at each other, until two of the bar stools come free and we launch ourselves gratefully at them – climbing aboard as if they're rafts and we're floating in a shipwrecked sea.

Considering the prices, I know I should make the rum last a bit longer. But in five minutes we're both finished. "What do you want?" I mouth, pointing to my purse and then to the bar in the international sign language of noisy clubs.

Dylan stops staring out at the dance floor, taps his glass and gives me the thumbs up.

I get us both a second double and Dylan drinks his and immediately orders another round, Black Russians this time. We drink and keep on watching the dance floor. Thud-thud-thud. Gyrate-gyrate-gyrate. It's like a different planet out there. Dylan leans over to talk into my ear. I shiver, even though it's about a million degrees in this place. "I feel like a non-swimmer looking at a pool full of people," he says. "I'm scared I might drown out there."

I smile and take his hand. "Maybe you just need to dive in."

Yikes, where did that come from? I must be kamikaze-trained on some deep subconscious level to say the exact opposite of what I mean. Or maybe I just know how much Dylan needs a friend.

He stares at the dance floor for a few more minutes, occasionally rocking forward on the bar stool like he's willing himself to take the plunge. Then he leans into me again. "Look, let's just get out of here and head over to Pete's, shall we?"

"You sure?" I ask. "What about. . .?"

Dylan shrugs. "Not my scene."

Fireworks explode behind my eyes. Yessity yes yes! "OK," I say, standing up and giving him a hug. "If you're sure."

"Thanks, Jen. You're an angel." He looks at me

blearily and I realize that the three doubles weren't the first drinks he's had tonight, that he was more than half-cut before we even set foot in the door – that explains all the staring out the window on the train. He pulls me into a hug. "You look beautiful tonight, babe. Come on, let's go."

I look beautiful. Babe. Let's go.

I burn the words into my memory for safe-keeping as we make for the door, arms around each other. My stomach's doing backflips of joy but then, with Machiavellian timing, "Music" comes on, capital M. Now, Dylan never misses an opportunity to dance to Madonna. It would be like blasphemy or something.

"One dance, just to this. Then we'll go."

Damn. Major backfire or what? Knowing we're off in five minutes seems to give him the courage to get up there. He grabs my hand and tries to pull me along with him. I resist, but then Madonna starts singing.

And I wake up. It's like a warning. Suddenly Madonna's standing right there in my mind, saying, *music makes the people come together, Jen. Do you want the people to come together?*

"No way, Madonna," I reply in my head, "not unless the people are me and Dylan."

"Well then," says Madonna, "what are you waiting for?"

I take a deep breath and let Dylan lead me into the crowd – double wobbly with the heels and the drink.

This is it – pistols at dawn for my man and my dream.

We dance really close together, just grinning and kind of pretending to be grooving ironically at first. But Madonna has this magical ability to make me feel like a total goddess and soon we're dancing for real, working our way into the middle of the floor, really getting into it. I feel like Pele and Morrigan and Venus all rolled into one.

It's perfect.

We're in the middle of this gay paradise and Dylan's not taking his eyes off me.

12

"But not *too* innocent, huh?"

"Wow, smells good in here," says Jase, strolling in. He's got a light jacket swung over his shoulder which he tosses on to the bench in the hall. "Nice pad."

He kisses me on the lips, just quickly, and it feels strangely awkward. Bollocks – I *knew* the wine glass and wooden spoon were overkill. It's horrible – like we're acting out some weird "honey, I'm home" sitcom that neither of us are cast right for. Damn. I should have ditched the pinny too. I decide to start plying him with alcohol, to distract him from the v unerotic happy families vibe.

"Drink?"

"Yeah, lovely."

He follows me into the kitchen and I can tell he's hanging back a bit to appreciate the boots and the skirt. Yep. The pain is well worth it.

I get another glass down and reach for the wine bottle.

"Got any beers?" says Jase.

Beers. Shit.

"No, I. . ." I say, flustered, and my hand stops halfway to the wine bottle.

Jase shrugs and grins. "No worries. Some vino'll do me fine."

I fill the glass and top up my own, feeling stupidly grateful that he's gone with the wine.

Then I remember that I'm supposed to be stirring the risotto and lunge for the pan, nearly knocking Jase's glass out of his hand. I haven't given it my *loving and undivided attention* for at least three minutes so I start stirring at triple speed, somehow hoping to make up for it.

Jase stands behind me and puts his arms round my waist.

My stomach flips over and my knees buckle. Thank God for the FMBs – they're virtually holding me up.

He puts his chin on my shoulder and peers into the pan. "What's that stuff?"

"Risotto. Wild Mushroom."

"Smells gorge. What meat is it?"

I stiffen. "Erm, there's no meat in this one, actually. It's a recipe."

"Oh, right. Still, looks good."

God dammit! If I ever meet Jamie Oliver I'm going to have his naked ass for this.

I know we should have the prawn cocktails now, but

I'm chained to the risotto and when *that's* ready you have to eat it as soon as possible. I wonder how soon is possible – for example, is it all right to leave it a few minutes while you have a prawn cocktail?

I test the rice, stir in the grated parmesan and decide that as soon as possible will have to be after the prawn cocktails – I didn't spend hours (well, OK, minutes) defrosting prawns and opening jars of sauce for nothing.

I hand Jase the wine bottle and nudge him through to the lounge/diner, grabbing the chilled bowls from the fridge as I go. As it turns out, I didn't need to worry about time. Jase scoffs his in two seconds flat and I follow suit. As I take the empty bowls back into the kitchen he runs his hands across my hips and it's like the prawns have come back to life and are doing a crazy calypso in my stomach.

The risotto's good too, though there are a few bits of grit in it I didn't get off the mushrooms. I pretend it's big bits of black pepper and I don't think Jase even notices. I lean down to unzip the boots before I thrombosify myself and one makes a rasping sound.

"Good one, Li!" goes Jase, chuckling.

Ohmigod! He thinks I just did a huge fart! I blush bright red, which makes me look really guilty. What's worse – admitting that I've got way too tight boots on just for him, or farting like a trooper in the middle of our posh dinner. Erm – no contest.

"It's the boots," I say. "They're a bit tight. I'm just unzipping them."

"Oh, yeah, right," says Jase, winking at me.

I take a deep breath and unzip the second one really fast, hoping this will magically make it sound completely different.

"The more you eats, the more you farts!" sings Jase.

"I didn't!" I say, a little sharply.

"I know! Just singing. Can't I sing if I want?" He's teasing me now.

"Course," I say, blushing.

God, normally I wouldn't care if I farted off the Richter scale. I'm really wound up this evening, probably all this slaving over a hot stove. But I suddenly realize it's not just the celery-choosing and the risotto-stirring. I'm nervous about sleeping with Jase.

God, that's a shock. That was the one thing about this whole evening I assumed I could handle. I tell myself that I don't have to do IT tonight if I'm not completely comfortable, that we can just go with the flow and see what happens. That takes the pressure off and I suddenly feel way more chilled.

Jase scoffs the risotto like he's one of his mum's stray dogs, and then goes out to the kitchen to get the leftovers too, even though I warn him about the eat as soon as possible business.

"Not so bothered about the no meat thing now, are you?" I tease.

"Too right. I wasn't sure about this stuff at first, but it's well tasty."

"Hey! You told me it looked nice!"

Jase shrugs. "Yeah, well. Didn't want to go upsetting my bird, did I?"

I grin at him and decide to ditch the posh dinner business. I'm not grown-up and I'm not romantic, so why keep it up when we get on better just being ourselves?

The wine level in the bottle's getting dangerously low and I start wishing I'd bought more bevvies. Maybe we could pop to the offie later for some vodka and tinnies. I won't have to worry about being underage with Jase there.

Jase has a fag on the patio (I make him go outside 'cause my mum's got a smoke-radar built into her head) then we drink the rest of the wine on the sofa, and eat half the chocolate cloud cake straight off the plate while watching the DVD that Jase brought round. It's really one long car chase with occasional huge explosions, but that's all right – neither of us are exactly following the plot anyway.

If ya know what I mean.

(In case you don't, by the time the credits come up we've snogged the living daylights out of each other and Jase has got my gorgeous new Goddess-Society-Approved black lacy bra undone under my shirt, which is hanging on by one button. I've got his shirt completely off and his belt undone, but I haven't put my hand down there yet. For the last half an hour we've been snogging with me on top, moving together, and I think I'm going to *explode* because even though it's through layers of material I can feel a *lot*.)

To think I might have gone to bed with Robbie Jones at Dez's party last year and missed having my first time with Jase. Thank God I went to bed with flu instead!

Because this. Is. A-mazing.

I mean, I've snogged boys from school before, and quite a lot more, if I'm honest, but it was nothing like this. This is hot and sticky and incredible – my whole body goes wild every time he moves. I didn't think your toes could get turned on, or your ears or whatever. But they can. And by the look on Jase's face, I know I'm totally doing it for him too.

I decide to go in for the killer blow, so to speak. I sit up on top of him and arch my eyebrow. I've been practising that for years and I finally get what it's for. Then I unbutton his jeans and start trying to get them down, but it's hard with his weight on them.

"One sec," he says, arching his back and sliding them off on to the floor.

I pull down his purple silk boxer shorts and – ping! – there it is. For a minute I'm completely thrown by the size of it, it seems soooooo massive. I spend about three seconds feeling really embarrassed and stupid and then Jase strokes my hair back from my face and groans which I find just so sexy I really get into it.

I can faintly hear the buzz of the fuzzy TV screen as I move. I shiver with pleasure as Jase groans things like "Jeez, Lia. Holy fuck you're good." Well, I should be – it's not the first blow job I've ever given. I ask myself fleetingly how I feel about actually having sex, but I'm not nervous any more. It doesn't seem like a different thing now – it's just another part of it all. Jase half sits up then, kisses the top of my head and slowly slides his hand up the side of my knickers.

Oh. My. God.

It's a rush to get the condom on after that. Lucky he has some in his jeans pocket, there's no way I'd make it upstairs for mine.

I can't really describe how it feels, to have him inside me. It's like nothing else. It hurts a bit, but only at first. We snog really hard and he grabs my hair and I bite his shoulder. But it's not separate actions, it's one whole thing. Then suddenly it's over, and I'm like, *is that it?* To be honest, I thought it might last a bit longer. You know, like maybe even a whole *minute*? But it was still great. Amazing. We lie there, knotted up in our half-off clothes, panting and kissing each other.

"Lia Harcourt, you are a bloody sex goddess."

I wallow in the smell of him, the feel of him. "Damn right I am. And that was only my first time too. I'm going to get better and better."

"Was I good enough then?"

"Oh, perfectly satisfactory," I say, biting my cheeks, "although there were a few minor points. . ."

"Cheeky mare! Still, nothing we can't put right on your second time, then. Or your third, or fourth, or. . ."

I roll into hugging him but he sits up. "Just a sec, darling. I need a slash and a fag."

Lucky I ditched the posh thing earlier, isn't it?

I hear the loo flush upstairs and Jase pads back down.

"I'm going for a shower," I say.

"OK," says Jase.

I think he might come with me but he just gets dressed and goes out for a smoke.

I go upstairs, strip off in the bathroom and get in the shower. I'm quite relieved he didn't come actually.

A bit of half-dressed candlelit sex on the sofa is one thing, but stark naked under the hundred-watt glare of the bathroom light is something else altogether. I take my time, going over all the details and thinking, *I've done it, I've done it, I've done it.*

I get dressed into my shirt and skirt again, and go downstairs in bare feet. The FMBs have done their job – for tonight anyway. I make us coffees and we sit outside on the patio bench, staring up at the moon. For some reason I want a cigarette too, so I nudge one out of the pack. I take a really deep drag like I see Jase do. Mistake. I cough it out, smoke coming out of my nose and mouth, making my eyes sting.

I hope my bright red face doesn't show in the dark. "I've never smoked before," I say, stating the bloody obvious.

Jase laughs, grinding out his finished fag on the flagstones and taking mine. "Well, don't start now, darling. I like my girls sweet and innocent."

"*Girls?*"

"You know what I mean. Girl. You."

I raise my eyebrow again (that is *such* a cool move). "But not too innocent, huh?"

"Not too innocent, no."

I kiss him full on the lips as he sweeps me off the bench, inside the house and up the stairs. And I'm not even wearing the FMBs.

13

"God, even the *drinks* are gay."

I only forget my mission for a second –
I've got too into the dancing – and
suddenly we're in a circle with a few other
people. I'm not too worried about it; well, maybe about
the redhead who keeps strutting her funky stuff in my
direction, but not about Dylan. A blond is checking
him out, but he's just into the music, and anyway, when
this song's over we're going to Pete's to get
cappuccinos and listen to acoustic guitar and talk
about films.

Aren't we?

I stop dead still and stare at Dylan. How did *that*
happen? A minute ago we were just part of this crowd
and now he's on Pulling: Level 1, full frontal dancing
really close to The Blond . . . and I'm nowhere and all
over the place.

Desperate times call for desperate measures. I go
into a mad frenzy of grooving and shimmy over to him.
Then it's like Dylan is the last seat on a packed train
and The Blond and me are jostling for it. Sadly, The

Blond wins. Dylan gives me a look like, *what the. . .?*, but I just go into an even crazier whirlwind of dancing, hoping to knock him out of The Blond's clutches by brute force. Seeing me coming, The Blond wraps himself more tightly round Dylan like a boa constrictor, but Dylan's not responding – instead he's just staring at me. I've won! Any second now he'll throw Snake Boy aside and take me in his arms and. . .

"Jen, are you OK?"

That's when I realize he's less thinking I'm the dancing queen and more thinking I'm having an epileptic fit. Then, just to perfect the moment, the wobbly heel snaps clean off Shelley's shoe. I lurch sideways, then spend an unpleasant minute or two scrabbling round at gyrating-crotch level in pools of spilt beer to get it back.

Rigid with embarrassment, I motion to Dylan that I'm fine and that I'm going to sit down. I could swear The Blond gives me a sly wink behind Dylan's back, although it might just be my crazed imagination. I hobble to the bar, trying to hold on to my last inch of dignity by tiptoeing on my right foot so no one'll notice the missing heel. I'm also wishing I'd asked Shelley how much these were before borrowing them. I probably owe her about three hundred and fifty quid.

So I'm sitting at the bar, the heel in my hand, trying to douse my burning jealousy with vodka. But everyone knows what happens if you throw alcohol on a fire. I keep taking furtive little looks at Dylan. Well, I think they're furtive but no doubt they're as obvious as if I'm a lighthouse with a big beam on my head, directed straight at him. The Blond is resting his arms on Dylan's shoulders as he dances. I'm sure he's looking so sickeningly sexy, tanned, and rhythmic *just* to piss me off. "Huh! Get any closer and you'll need a condom," I bitch, as The Blond nudges his leg right in between Dylan's thighs.

"Ohh, me-ow!" says a voice beside me. I turn round, expecting to see a girl. Even a guy would do. But this person seems to be both, and neither.

He, or should I say "she"? extends a manicured hand. "I'm Nicola. Nicola Start."

I giggle despite my misery. Nicola Start. Nickerless Tart. "Oh, yeah, right, I get it. I'm Jen."

Nicola makes air-kissing motions in my direction from her bar stool. "*Enchanté.* Here." She holds out her hand and I go to shake it, but then she waves her fingers towards the heel. I'm so confused I hand it over without question.

Nicola rummages in his – sorry – *her* handbag and whips out a little tube of superglue. The surprise must show on my face, because she says, "I keep it handy for sticking sequins back on. I lost a heel once too – that was before I caught on to these special shoes that are designed to take more weight." She

143

extends a muscular leg and foot and waggles her toes in their turquoise sequinned sandals.

"They're lovely," I say lamely, watching her expertly squeezing the glue out like Handy Andy. I've got a pretty vivid imagination, but I have to admit that sitting at a bar in a gay club having my heel stuck back on by a huge drag queen with a trick name isn't something I saw happening in my life. Not for a good few years, anyway.

"Leg, sweetie."

I think I've forfeited the right to ever worry about how I look after turning into crazy tornado girl on the dance floor, so I hoick my leg up on to the edge of Nicola's bar stool, and she sticks the heel back on the shoe.

Because of the weird angle, my foot in the shoe suddenly looks like it's not part of me at all. An image flashes up in my mind of Mum on her knees on the chunky old quarry tiles, the heels of her silver sandals pointing into the air. Was that *the* night?

Then Nicola says, "Oooh, Valentino, very nice!" and I snap back into the present. "With the little clip-on jewels too! I'd love some of those but they don't do my size."

"Too bad," I say weakly.

Nicola's holding the heel on while the glue dries. Holding *very firmly*.

I giggle nervously. "You may have the gold lamé and

ultra-volume mascara of a woman, but you've got the iron grip of a sheep-shearing Scotsman."

Nicola just gives me a reproachful look through her fan of eyelashes. I blush – maybe you're not meant to mention the *man* aspect.

"How do you get your legs so smooth?" she says.

"Oh, it's just those disposable waxing strips."

She's smiling again. "I'll have to give those a try." We're obviously on safer ground with girly topics.

She lets go of my ankle, which returns to its normal colour as the blood rushes back. Then she tries waggling the heel. "All fixed, honey." I grin and mentally stick the three hundred-odd quid back in my savings account. "But don't step on it for half an hour. It still needs to get hard. It's no good unless it's rock solid, ya know?" She gives me a conspiratorial wink.

I desperately try to act like she's just talking about the heel, but my beetroot face gives me away. "Thanks so much. You're my fairy godmother."

Nicola tosses her curly black locks and gestures at the dance floor. "And now, Cinderella, you shall go to the ball! When the glue's dried, anyway."

I smile. "Thanks, but I've already been and it sucks. The princes only have eyes for each other."

Nicola pats my hand. "I'm afraid I don't have a magic spell for prince trouble, sweetie." Just then someone calls to her from across the bar. Another *lady*. "Oh, there's Evita," she says, air-kissing near me again. "See you later, darling."

"See you. And thanks for the glue!"

Nicola smiles dazzlingly and sashays off, and after a while I sense someone else sitting down on the stool next to me. I turn and see the girl who was checking me out on the dance floor. She says, "Hi, can I buy you a drink?"

I look at her wearily, and blearily. She must have missed the washing machine on spin-cycle incident – either that or she's nuts herself and thinks we'd make a good pair. I don't have the energy to be either rude or polite, so I just say, "No thanks."

"Oh, sorry, are you with someone?"

"No, why? Why would I be? I'm not a lesbian," I scowl.

"Ooh, ex-cuuuuse *me*," she says all sarcastically. "God knows what came over me. Maybe it's the way you're all dressed up, sitting in a gay club, that I thought you might be, you know, *gay* – but that's obviously some crazy idea I got."

"I'm sorry." I hold out my hand. "I'm Jen."

"Donna," she says, squeezing it. "And I'm sorry, too. You're a real hottie."

Shock must have registered on my face because Donna laughs and says, "God, didn't you notice every girl in the place giving you the look-see when you came in?"

146

Well, it's sad to admit, but I was really chuffed about that. Back in hetero-land I'm not a hottie. Usually I'm only a lukewarmy, and quite often I feel like a wet Wednesday.

I smile. "Thanks. You've cheered me up. I'll get the drinks."

We get margaritas, which come with little pink plastic flowers in. God, even the *drinks* are gay.

"So, why *are* you here, then?" Donna asks. "I mean, a lot of straights come for the music and the atmosphere. But you don't look in the mood for either."

"Long boring story," I mumble. "Summary: I've been in love with my best friend Dylan for like, ever. I was just about to tell him when he came out with. . . Well, let's just say he came out. I was devastated, heartbroken et cetera. So I thought the best thing to do was get dressed up, come down here, show him what he's missing. Which would have been fine, if it wasn't for The Blond," I spit, like a wife about a mistress.

Donna follows my baleful glance and clocks Dylan, who has graduated to Pulling: Level 2 – the drink-and-sofa-and-"oooohh, everything you say is soooooooo witty" bit.

"Well, at least someone got what they came for," I drawl, taking a great slug of my drink. I almost choke, partly because the salt and sour has hit the back of my throat but mostly because The Blond has just slung his arm casually round Dylan's shoulders, using the old

"I feel like a stretch" manoeuvre. Utterly corny, but deadly effective.

Donna grimaces. "My condolences," she says, as if my favourite aunt has just died, rather than all my hopes and dreams. "Still, if it's any consolation, it's not you. It's just that people are how they are, yeah? I've known I was gay since I was about ten. I'll bet Dylan has too. There's nothing more you can do – you've given it your best shot." She gives me a lingering look and goes, "Phew! You sure have!"

"Oi, eyes off!" I joke. Then, "And no, that's no consolation at all. What I need is a magic wand."

Donna laughs. "Yeah, a pink one about eight inches long."

I giggle despite myself, and look over at Dylan for the gazillionth time.

The Blond obviously has a magic wand, because Dylan has moved on to Pulling: Level 3 – tonsil tennis. I think about how I was the last person to kiss those delicious lips and a wave of self-pity washes over me. "He was it for me, you know?" I groan. "I wanted to be with him. I wanted *it* to be with him. I'm doomed to be a virgin for ever."

Donna grins. "Join the club."

"Really?"

"Technically, yeah."

"Thanks for the support, but technically doesn't count."

I'm just getting up the guts to ask her something I've always wondered – what lesbians actually *do* in bed, when I see Dylan and The Blond stand up. They interlock fingers (yuck!) and start weaving through the crowd. Good. It's about time they came and talked to me. I know Dylan was only hanging out over there because he saw I was chatting to someone and not on my own. But even so, it was starting to get a bit rude. There's no way Dylan'll let The Blond come to Pete's with us. He's probably just coming over to get another drink or something. Maybe I can buy him one. How about a cyanide and Coke?

But when I catch Dylan's eye, my dark thoughts melt away and I can't help beaming. Coffee and guitar here we come. Only, my smile fixes on my face as I realize The Blond isn't heading for the bar at all – and nor is Dylan.

They're heading for the door.

Our eyes meet again and Dylan seems to take my psychotic-clown grin as a "go forth and shag thy catch" encouraging smile. He gives me a thumbs up and I think about what that means in diving. Going up. He should do it the other way – *going down*. God, I really am an expert in self-torture, aren't I? I gulp the rest of my drink to try and sluice away the steamy, sweaty, squelchy scenes unfolding in my imagination. It works, but I wish it hadn't.

I should have stayed focussed on the gory detail

because when that fades then the bigger picture hits me like a tidal wave. Dylan isn't just fooling around for a bit in the club. He isn't just having a laugh for half an hour when he can see I'm talking to someone anyway.

He's leaving without even coming over to say goodbye.

He's leaving without *me*.

That hurts so much I get an actual pain in my chest, which makes me breathe in sharply.

"You OK?" asks Donna.

I pull myself together just enough to smile and slide down from the bar stool. "Yeah . . . it's probably just the heat. Well, looks like I'm off stooge duty for tonight. Good to meet you."

"Yeah, you too," she says. "Thanks for the drink. And hey, don't worry, you'll find the one for you."

"I already have, that's the problem," I mutter as I weave my way towards the loos.

I spend ten minutes in a cubicle – that's one minute having a pee and nine minutes just lingering, with absolutely no idea what to do next. I told the girls me and Dylan were getting together tonight. OK, it's true it wasn't me who actually said it was a date – but I didn't set them straight either. I still can't work out how it's gone so wrong. I'm sure this gay thing is just a phase – after all, Dylan and I are meant for each other. I really thought the universe would support me if I took a risk.

I thought the goddesses would make it come out right. I thought Mum would help me too, from the other side. It's not just about Dylan. It's about my whole faith in being alive. I knew one hundred per cent this was going to happen and it hasn't. It's broken everything apart. I don't feel like *me* any more.

I collect my coat and get out of the club and just start walking. There are a few drops of rain in the air, but I hardly notice. I turn into a little back street and that's when the tears come, nearly choking me. I just pace faster, trying to get away from all the crazy feelings twisting inside me. I've got no idea where I'm headed – but one thing's for sure – there's no way I'm going home. Not to the empty house that I so carefully got Nan out of for my night with Dylan. Not to the new purple bedspread he noticed on his last visit. And not to the girls, who'll hate me when they find out what a complete lying fantasist I am.

I just don't know what to think. About anything.

My feet are slipping painfully inside Shelley's shoes, but I keep walking, until my heels are actually raw and bleeding and I *have* to stop. I take the shoes off, tie the straps round the handle of my bag and carry on. It starts spitting and then lashing down. I spot a cab with its light on coming my way and stick my arm out. As it veers towards me, slowing, I step off the pavement and walk right in front of it, staring straight ahead. There's a squeal of wet brakes as the cab skids to a stop, only just missing me, then a blast of the horn. I don't see the driver's face, don't think about what he's thinking, or how he feels. I don't see or think or feel anything myself. The only thing that dimly registers is that I'm still alive, so I hitch my bag further on to my shoulder, and keep right on walking.

14

"It's meant to be my sexy voice, OK?"

Paul was so surprised when I hailed a cab outside the restaurant without giving him more than a peck on the cheek. I bet I'm the only girl who's ever told him they're cabbing it home at the end of the night and then actually *does*.

I check my make-up as we roll slowly over Waterloo Bridge and through Elephant and Castle. I practise my sexy voice as we sail through Forest Hill and Sydenham. When we get to Beckenham I give the driver the address.

Not mine. Stick's.

Climbing through his window's pretty tricky. I curse my gangly legs – it's like trying to get Bambi into a swimsuit. Thank God his room's in the basement. His parents are safely tucked up in bed two floors up. At least, I hope they are.

It's only just past eleven and I fully expect him to be out with Hector and Crispin and his other freakishly named mates from school. I have a moment of panic thinking what if he's out with the *someone* girl and he

153

brings her back and here I am, as per my plan. The thought freezes me for a moment, half in and half out of the window, but I force myself to clamber through. I always get what I want ... and this won't be any different. Please, God, don't let this be any different.

When I finally tumble into the room, dragging my purple bag behind me, I'm surprised (but relieved) to see that Stick's there, *alone*. He's sprawled out asleep on top of the bedcovers, surrounded by a pile of records and his laptop. I slide the records across the bed – it's like playing Operation, getting them off without waking him up – and stack them neatly in the corner. Shifting the laptop sets the bloody thing going and it does its start-up music really loud. Shit! I stand stock-still, smothering it with my coat while Stick twitches and sprawls a bit more. This could spoil my whole plan – if he wakes up now he'll just think I'm stealing his computer. When I'm sure he's properly back asleep, I take off my boots and jeans and leather coat and top to reveal my Goddess-Society-Approved purple lacy bra and thong. Then I feel the chill from the window so I put the coat back on. Next I get out my Box of Tricks and start work.

In a few minutes, everything's ready.

Stick's going to wake up gently to flickering candlelight, the heady aphrodisiac aromas of jasmine and ylang ylang and the sound of Norah Jones playing softly on the stereo.

Bollocks, no he's not.

I've put one of the candles too near the bed, so instead he shoots bolt upright to the smell of burning duvet and the sound of me swearing unerotically whilst whipping the bloody thing out from under him, shoving my red boots back on and jumping up and down on it. Damn! The only thing that was meant to be schmokin' was me!

"Shelley, what the hell are you doing?" Stick hisses.

"Saving your life!" I grunt, crushing out the last embers. Thank Christ I didn't wear my sandals – I'd've ended up with flame-grilled toes.

"Oh. Right. And you're dressed like a hooker because. . .?"

"A hooker!" I'm about to slap him one when I catch a glimpse of myself in his mirror. I have to admit that the underwear with just the coat and boots *is* more Sunset Strip than La Senza. "It was chilly, and then I had to stamp out the fire. . ." I say huskily, suddenly remembering to use the sexy voice I was practising in the taxi.

"And why do you sound like that?" he mumbles, rubbing his eyes.

"Like what?"

"Like Billie Holiday. Have you been smoking some harsh weed?" He looks genuinely puzzled.

I'm going to try bluffing it, but the romantic mood's already wrecked so I just go, "Shut up, Stick. It's meant to be my sexy voice, OK?"

"So . . . why *are* you here in the middle of the night setting fire to me and talking in a sexy voice?"

Jeez! Do I have to spell it out? I give him a look and say, "Why do you think?"

"I don't know! Maybe you're going to sacrifice me or something." He squints at me, confused. "Is this some new thing of Jen's?"

Obviously I *do* have to spell it out. "Not sacrifice you. Seduce you."

Stick stares at me. *"Oh."*

I sit on the bed, lean over and let my coat fall open a little further, so he gets the full effect of the purple lacy extravaganza. "Do you like my underwear?" I say.

"The knickers are a little weird," says Stick, "but then, you're more up on fashion than me."

"What's wrong with them?" I ask, craning my neck to look down at the tiny lacy thong.

"Oh, I, er," says Stick, trying desperately to cover up a snort of laughter. "I was talking about the ones on your head. But the ones on your backside are really nice too."

Forget axe-murderers and vampires and all that. This is the stuff *real* horror movies are made of.

"Oh. My. God." I shriek. "I just tied my hair up with them to go in the shower. I've been out in the West End like this!" We stare at each other, and then we both burst into absolute hysterics. Mascara tears run down

156

my face and I'm probably going to rupture something vital, but I just can't stop.

"No wonder people were staring at me," I wheeze. "Ha! I just thought it was 'cause I looked so sexy! Really it was because . . . because. . ." I collapse back into giggles.

"You know what's worse?" says Stick. "The label's sticking out! You've been going round with, *size 8–10 – Wash dark colours separately* on your head!"

"Noooooooooo!"

I pull the knickers out of my hair and start swatting him with them. God, I hope Paul didn't notice. Actually, I don't care if he did. Stick grabs my wrists and pulls me down on to the bed. Our faces are an inch away from each other, panting and grinning, but then suddenly the smiles fall away and our eyes lock, intense. I lean down and kiss him full on the mouth.

But he doesn't kiss me back. "Shel, you know I really like you. . ."

"And I *really* like you," I say, kissing him again, this time tasting my own lipstick on his lips.

"But, what I mean is, we're mates. . . I think this would mess it up. . ."

"No, it wouldn't," I say, running my fingers down his spine. Stick sort of groans and swallows hard. So I'm not his type, huh? *Beg to differ.* "Now shut up and kiss me."

"OK, look, I wasn't going to say this, but maybe I

157

should be honest. I don't want to be just another guy to you."

That stops me in my tracks. Stick thinks I sleep with people all the time. He thinks this is just a booty call 'cause late night Buffy's been cancelled or something. Char-ming!

"Stick! You're not just another guy. You're THE guy. I'm still a virgin."

He does this kind of half-laughing, half-choking thing.

"*Really*," I say, handing him my last scrap of dignity. "But not for long. You're the one I want to lose it with. Now."

I run my fingertips up his right thigh, right to the hem of his boxers. I know that's unfair tactics, but I've put my heart on the line now. This *has* to work out.

"You want to lose it with me?" Stick marvels. "I thought you'd done it ages ago. But you're here and you want it to be with me?"

"Yes." I pull him close and kiss him hard on the lips. He kisses me back. It's strange because it's Stick and yet it feels completely natural too, like it *should* be Stick.

"Wow," he says. I know he feels as hot for me as I do for him. I know because the evidence is poking into my thigh. I wriggle my fingers under the elastic of his boxer shorts and take hold of the evidence and. . .

"Oh, God," Stick groans, clearly in some kind of

penis heaven. But then he pulls away. "Listen, maybe it's not a cool thing for a guy to admit, but I've gotta tell you 'cause it might make you change your mind. The thing is. . . I'm still one too."

The half-laughing, half-choking thingy must be contagious 'cause I start doing it too. "You're still a virgin? But. . ."

I swear I could barbecue hotdogs on Stick's cheeks.

"Yeah. I'm actually pretty crap with girls. I freeze up and get all sarky and that. You're the only one of the species I've ever really been able to talk to."

"Well, that's good, 'cause I'm the only one you need to worry about."

"So you don't mind?"

"Course not."

I kiss him hard on the lips again and that's it. No more talking.

When I wake up the next morning it takes me a moment to remember where I am. Then when I do I get this big grin all over my face. I'm with Stick and I'm an ex-virgin!

I kiss him awake and he leans into me and starts kissing me back. Then he seems to come to, and pushes me away. "Hey, I don't think this is a good idea," he says.

I blink at him. "Hello? You're a guy, remember?"

Stick smiles shyly. "After you fell asleep I lay here

thinking about something. And it's cool if you don't want to, but. . . Well, I want to be with you. Not just for sex. I want you to be my girlfriend."

"I thought I wasn't your type," I tease.

Stick looks perplexed. "Oh, come on, Shel, I just came out with that 'cause you didn't fancy *me*."

"You *thought* I didn't."

"Well, what were you saying at Jen's then?"

I blush. "Nothing. I was just being an idiot. But it's sorted now. I'd love to be your girlfriend."

A long, slow kiss seals the deal. But then I remember something. Or rather, *someone*. "Hang on, don't you already *have* a girlfriend?"

It's Stick's turn to look bashful now. "Nope," he says.

"But what about Miss Whatserface, the goth-metal princess of darkness?"

"Oh, I erm, I made her up."

"You made her *up*?"

"Yeah, she's completely fabricado. I was so gutted about what you said I had to face it out somehow."

I hug him tight and giggle. "What the hell were you going to do about the gig?"

"God knows. I hadn't exactly thought it through, had I? Maybe they have rent-a-fake-girlfriend companies in the Yellow Pages."

"You muppet!"

Stick grabs my arms and pushes me back into the pillows. "You'll get a slap for that."

"Ooh, yes please!"

We tumble around in the bed, laughing and snogging. I get so turned on that I slink down under the covers and start doing some Madonna-with-a-bottle-style deep throat on him. Stick makes a sort of strangled surprised noise.

"Good morning, love!" Oh. My. God. That must be Stick's mum with his cup of tea and the *NME*. Now *she* makes a sort of strangled surprised noise. "Oh, my goodness, I'm so. . . Excuse me, I erm. . . I never would have. . . But you've never brought anyone back before. . ."

Stick's not saying anything. Well, what the hell *do* you say in this situation?

For a minute I seriously consider living the rest of my life under these bed covers. But, although I'm dying of embarrassment too I decide to face it out. Sophia's obviously shocked enough to see the lump in the bed, but she's going to get the surprise of her life when she sees it's me. I slide back up the bed and pop my head out of the duvet.

"Shelley!" she half-screams. "Erm, hello, dear. Lovely to see you as always. It's a change to see you, erm, not quite so . . . dressed as usual, but. . ." She takes a deep breath and grips the doorframe. "Would you like a drink? I mean, can I get you. . .? No, maybe not. I'll, erm, come back later, or not. . ."

As she backs out through the door Stick groans and I collapse into laughter.

"She looked so shocked!" I gasp.

"I know! Maybe she'll finally start knocking now. She'll be well chuffed we're together, though. She knows how I feel about you. She's been on at me about making a move for months."

"Really?"

"Too right. I've been imagining this for ages, though it didn't include you breaking into my room with a pair of kaks in your hair and setting the bed on fire. Or giving my mum a full-on porno show, come to mention it."

I know I should laugh but I suddenly feel deflated. "It was your first time too and I messed it up, didn't I?"

"*What?* No way! Actually, I thought those were your finest moments!" Stick wraps his arms round me and pulls me close. "I don't want the dream, Shel. I want the reality. I want you, babe."

"You got me." I smile and kiss him and do my killer stroke right up his thigh again. I'm pleased to see that it has the same effect as last night. "You know you can't lose two virginities in one time, don't you?" I say, teasing him. "You've still got yours!"

"You've still got *yours*, more like!"

"No way! I've checked. Mine definitely went just after the chocolate body paint ran out. But what are we going to do about you?"

"How about you show me what's what, oh hugely experienced sex goddess?" says Stick, running his fingers lightly across my nipples.

Oooh, mama.

But then he sees the clock. "Oh, shit!" he cries, leaping up. "It's half eight! I've gotta go!"

"What? Where?"

"Record fair in Camden. I've arranged to see a couple of people about some indie rares I'm after. Shit! Shit!" He hops about trying to get his legs into his trousers.

He must see the look on my face 'cause he sits back down on the edge of the bed and takes my hand. "Oh, Shel, I'm sorry. I know it's our first morning together, and. . . But it's like, if you don't get there early. . ."

I smile and put a finger to his lips. "I'm just hurt you don't want me to come."

"Come? That'd be brilliant. I just thought you'd be busy, you know, like usual. . ."

"Naa. No more schoolwork, remember? Besides, I'm your girlfriend and your girlfriend would come, right?"

Stick's grin is so gorgeous, I just want to pull him back into the bed again, but I resist. This record stuff's really important to him. "Just give me twenty seconds to dive in the shower. We can pick up my car while we're in town."

As I wrap my leather coat round me, step into my red boots and make for the bathroom, Stick says, "What's your car doing in town?"

I start – I'd forgotten all about Paul. I realize that Stick must never, *ever* find out about my original plan. Thank God I didn't mention it in the Studio when I got that text. At the time I didn't know why I hid it from Stick. I guess I know now. "Oh, *very* long, *very* boring story," I say, rolling my eyes, "to do with parking."

We get to Camden pretty much on time. Stick is seriously scary when he's doing business – he won't give an inch. Standing next to him, I felt like a mafia wife. We go round the market afterwards and instead of linking arms, like usual, we hold hands. Camden's much more Jen's thing than mine, but it's so great to be there with Stick. I keep saying it in my head – "I'm Stick's girlfriend." "Hi, I'm Shelley. I'm with Stick." "Yeah, did you know, Stick's got a new girlfriend? Me." It's weird, but cool.

We stop for cappuccinos in this little café over the lock and this time when Stick leans towards me over the table I'm certain he's going to kiss me. He doesn't get why it makes me laugh so much when he just brushes a bit of chocolate powder off my cheek. I'm about to explain about the Great Lily Pad Café Kiss Debate when my mobile goes off.

The minute Lia opens her mouth I know there's

something wrong. "Dylan just called," she says, breathless. "He's been ringing Jen's all morning to check she got back OK but she's not answering."

"But I thought he was with her."

"No, he went home with someone else last night and. . ."

"*He went home with someone else?*" I repeat. "He was on a date with Jen, for God's sake, and he goes home with some bird?!"

Lia's voice is thick with panic. "That's not the half of it, Shel. It wasn't a girl, it was a bloke. It was a gay club. Dylan doesn't even seem to know Jen thought it was a date."

I just stare at Stick. He's staring back, like, *what the hell is going on?*

"Shel?" says Lia. "I'm scared. I. . ."

I'm scared too. It seems completely crazy. Impossible. But if it's true then God only knows what state Jen was in when she left that club. I make my voice deliberately slow and calm. "Go over there and try to find out whether she's not in or just not answering. I'll be there as soon as I can," I say and hang up.

Stick's looking really concerned. "Shel, what's—"

"We need to get back," I say, grabbing my bag. "Now."

15

"You know, pledge your allegiance to the furry cup."

Jase had just left when Dylan called me. I couldn't believe what he was saying at first. It's so not like him to just go home and leave Jen on her own. And on her own in a gay club, too! I mean, true, Jen didn't go into any details about the date and that, but we assumed she was just being cagey like usual . . . and she didn't set us straight. God, she must have been so upset.

But I can't think about that now. I'm standing outside her house, pacing up and down between the front door and the big bay window. I've already given up ringing the doorbell. There's a little gap in the living room curtains – she's not in there but I keep thinking maybe she doesn't know about the gap and she'll walk past there and then I'll see she's all right. But what if she's not there at all? I march up and down between the house and the main road, looking out for Shelley's car.

Eventually, I run out of ideas and sit down on the front steps to wait for Shelley. I really don't think Jen's here. But where else can she be?

My mind races through the possibilities for the hundredth time. What if she met someone at the club and went home with him? But that's just not Jen. Even if she did, she'd have left a message for me or Shel. I mean, look what she was like about *me* being safe and that was in my own house!

She just wouldn't do something stupid like that anyway.

But what if she didn't know what she was doing? What if she got so out of her head she just went with someone and. . .? Or what if, *oh my God*, you read about these date-rape drugs, don't you? Jen does insist on getting drinks in a glass rather than swigging from a bottle, which is safer so long as you never put it down. And what if she didn't have enough money for a black cab and she got in some shonky taxi and . . . and. . .

What, Lia? says a little voice in the back of my head. *Go on, think it. Mugged? Raped? Murdered? Floating in the Thames?*

"Shut up!" I shout.

I'm almost out of my mind with worry when Shelley finally pulls up. She parks skew-whiff to the kerb and comes dashing down the drive. I fall into her arms and burst into tears.

"Oh, Lia, I'm so sorry. I was in Camden. Have you rung the bell?"

"Course I've rung the fucking bell!" I scream. "What the hell do you think I've been doing for the last hour? I've been going crazy thinking all these awful things. . ."

Shelley hugs me hard again. "Lia, calm down. It's OK. We can't sort this out if we're off our heads with panic. There's probably some completely simple explanation."

"Yeah, you're right," I say, but it's obvious that neither of us believe it.

"OK, let's think," says Shelley. "The curtains are still shut. So maybe she hasn't been back. There's no way she could have slept through the phone and the doorbell."

"Not the way I was bloody ringing it she couldn't!" I turn to the house in general and yell, "Jen! Jen! Are you in there? We're really worried!"

Nothing.

Then Shelley notices it and points. Jen's bedroom window, at the top of the house, is open a little bit. Now, Jen's madly security conscious and there's no way she'd leave any windows open if she was going out for the night. Even on the second floor.

"At least she's *been* home," says Shel. "Maybe she went out early. Come on, let's try the park."

"But what if she's in there but she can't answer?" I whisper, getting the Number One Dark Thought that's been looming at the back of my mind out at last. "She must have been in some kind of fantasyland about Dylan, to let us think it was a date. And she's always

168

been a bit weird 'cause of what happened to her mum. What if. . .?"

Shelley seems to steel herself. "Did you tell Dylan how she feels about him?" she asks.

"Course not."

Determinedly, Shelley shouts up at the half-open window. "Jen? Look, we know about Dylan. I mean, about it not really being a date. We know that he's gay and we know you're in love with him and I'm sorry but we're worried sick so, if you don't let us in, I'm going to ring him up this minute and tell him exactly how you feel. . ."

Next door's curtains are twitching. I catch a glimpse of Mrs Number Twelve – you know, scary nurse outfit and handcuffs woman from my mum's party. I'm about to give her the finger when Shelley nudges me and gestures up at Jen's window. *Her* curtains are twitching too. Suddenly a pale little hand parts them and a bunch of keys falls and hits the ground in front of us.

"Thank God for that!" I mutter, feeling my insides unclench.

We let ourselves in and bomb up the stairs. On the first floor, the bath's running. I poke my head round the bathroom door as we pass, but there don't seem to be any razor blades waiting on the side or anything. Not that you'd lay them out there with your face pack and. . . Oh, God, I'm so worried I don't know what I'm thinking.

We meet Jen on the stairs to her room. She's still in last night's clothes. Her feet are all filthy and cut, and her face is streaked with black mascara tears.

"You look like absolute shit, Jen!" I say, pulling her into a fierce hug. She freezes in my arms.

"Oh, that's because I only got in about seven," she says casually.

"What the hell were you doing? Not answering the phone or the door!" I yell, angry with her for acting so cool.

"We were really worried," says Shel. "And so was Dylan!"

"As if he would care," says Jen, pushing past us down the stairs. She gets about two steps, collapses against the wall, and starts crying her heart out.

She lets us hug her then, and we all just stand there, huddled up on the slim, curved steps.

"I thought you'd hate me," she says, between sobs. "Because it wasn't really a date and I told you. . ."

"No, you didn't. We assumed," Shel says firmly. "That's not your fault." She makes Jen look at her. "You have to trust us, Jen. We're your mates. You can tell us anything. Everything. We'll never judge you, will we, Li?"

"No way."

"Sometimes I want to," whispers Jen, wiping her nose with a tissue Shel's handed her. "I try, but the words just won't come out. And with Dylan I. . . I thought. . ."

"Oh, Jen, you half-believed it was a date yourself, didn't you?" I say.

Jen nods miserably and bursts into fresh tears. Me and Shel hug her tight again.

"Oh, God, and I encouraged you," goes Shel. "I honestly believed he liked you."

"He does," sniffles Jen. "He *loves* me. Just not in the way I want him to."

After a while we remember about the bath and Shel goes to turn it off. Jen lets me walk her slowly along the hall and put her in with a nice load of bubbles.

Shel calls Dylan and says in a false cheerful voice that Jen's here and fine, that she was just out in the park and that she can't talk now 'cause she's in the bath. She also says that Jen's sorry she worried him and she hopes he had a good night. Then she brings up three mugs of peppermint tea on a tray. We sit round in the bathroom, watching the steam on our tea rise with the steam of Jen's bath. We try not to look at her too much, in case it makes her uncomfortable. We know she won't talk till she's ready.

"I didn't know where to go after he left," she says at last, when the water's stopped steaming and the tea's all gone. "I just started walking, round Soho and Covent Garden. I ended up down by Charing Cross, so I went and stood on Hungerford Bridge."

"You weren't going to jump off, were you?" I say.

Shel gives me one of her looks but sadly it's too late to shut my famous trap. "Sorry," I say, and stare into my empty mug.

"I just stood there looking down at the water for hours. It must have been about four o'clock when this creepy man came along and started making, erm, 'lewd suggestions' I think it's called, so I ran all the way up to Pete's and stayed put until the tubes and that started up again about six."

"God, Jen, you should have gone to the police!" goes Shel.

"I couldn't face it. He was just some dickless wonder, no harm really."

"Yeah, they start like that but then they go on to child molesting and seriously sicko stuff," I say. "You should have reported it, you know."

Jen looks wearily at me and I realize that in the scale of how she's currently feeling a raving sex pervert coming on to her on Hungerford Bridge at four in the morning is just a minor inconvenience. *Jesus Christ.*

"I'm sorry about you and Dylan," says Shel, really quietly. "He doesn't seem gay at all."

"No, he just doesn't seem *camp* at all," says Jen. "There's a difference."

I frown at her. I just don't get it. "But weren't there any signs?"

Jen sighs deeply. "How would I know? Dylan's always

172

just been Dylan. But he's been out with girls before, so no, I guess not. . ."

I can tell she's uncomfortable talking about it, so I make myself back off. "I'm just sorry about it, that's all."

"Me too," says Shel.

"Me three," says Jen. And with just two words, she closes the entire subject. "But hey, how were *your* big nights?"

"Oh, you know, so so," goes Shel.

"All right I s'pose," I mumble.

"Oh, come on, girls, you don't have to be miserable for me. I'll sort my head out. God knows how, but. . . Look, really, fill me in. I could do with some good news."

So I tell them about me and Jase and then Shelley tells us about her and Stick.

That's right, *Stick*.

I do a big exaggerated double-take. "What?! I mean, *holy crap, Batman!* After you said all that stuff about *no way would I lose it with Stick* and – *hello?* – what the hell happened to Paul?"

She smiles. "I worked out that I was on the wrong track with him," she says, "and once I knew what I wanted, nothing was going to stop me getting it. So, after a bit of midnight housebreaking and some persuasion that was a little – shall we say – *below the belt*, I got my wicked way with Stick. *Not his type*, my ass!"

Like I said, I'm well surprised but Jen just smiles knowingly at her. The aromatherapy bath foam must be doing the trick 'cause she's even starting to look less like a crazy bag lady and more like her usual wise and mysterious self. "You went with your heart in the end," she says, "that's the mark of a true goddess."

Shel gapes at her. "In the *end*? You mean you knew I wanted Stick all along? So what was all that stuff about it just being my ego?"

I gape at her too. That's totally what *I* thought it was!

Jen smiles. "That was my challenge. You were supposed to go, 'That's rubbish, Jen. It's because I'm in love with him.'"

"Oh, I'm in love with him now, am I?" says Shel, looking incredulous.

Jen just smiles wanly.

Shelley claps her hand across her mouth. "Jeez, you're right! I'm in love with Stick! Oh. My. God!"

I can't help laughing. Now she says it, even I can see it was completely obvious all along.

"How about me?" I say. "Has the Prophetess Of The Sacred Bathtub got the gospel on me and Jase?"

Jen's eyes flicker for a moment. "Yes, you're in lust, darling. Just don't take it too seriously."

"No danger of that," I promise. "With us, it's just rampant sex and car-chase videos and that's the way I like it."

"What the hell was I thinking? Paul is so *shallow*!" says Shel suddenly. "The worst bit was when I was virtually passing out with boredom and he took my hand across the table and he said, 'You know, Shel, this is so great. I feel like I can really open up to you.' And I thought, Sweet Lord, if this is opening up, what's being cagey?!"

"Wow," I go. "You might actually be more of a *deep and meaningful* person than I thought, Shelley Green."

Shel cuffs me over the head. "Shut up, rampant sex girl, or I'll have those FMBs back!"

"Sorry, my lovely friendy-wendy. Me and the killer boots have got a hot date with Jase tomorrow. A nature walk in the park."

"Since when were you into nature?" asks Jen.

"Since precisely nine forty-two this morning, after our third, no, fourth, shag, when Jase told me about this secret bushy bit you can't see into from the path."

"Very non-tacky," says Jen. "Very Goddess Society, I *don't* think. So I guess all our good intentions went out the window then?"

"But what could be more wholesome?" I argue. "The paries are always on at me to get some fresh air and exercise."

Jen just rolls her eyes. "Shelley, you honoured the Goddess Society rules, didn't you?" she says. "I mean, *true love* on your first time! Come on, tell me something romantic and beautiful and non-tacky. I need it after that very low lowdown from Lia."

I stick my tongue out at her and Shel wrinkles her nose up. "Sorry, can't help you there. I nearly burnt Stick alive, and apparently I looked like a hooker and . . . oh, yeah, I had a pair of knickers in my hair."

Me and Jen dissolve into giggles. "The Goddess Society is in tatters," she cries dramatically. "I'm the only one who can save it, and there's not much chance of that now, is there?"

She starts looking all forlorn again, so I try to veer the subject away from Dylan. "Anyway, it can't possibly be tacky, wherever we do it, because Jase said he thinks I'm a sex goddess."

Shelley's eyes widen. "Really? Stick said that about me, too."

"No one's ever going to call me a sex goddess," wails Jen. "Which is ironic, because I'm the only one left in the Goddess Society."

"No, you're not," says Shel. "We're all members until we're all not."

"It's OK," says Jen. "You don't have to hang around for me. I'm going to start a new society anyway. How about the Ya Ya Spinsterhood?"

"Was that a joke?" I say. "That's good. Jokes are good. See, things are looking up already."

"It's not all that funny though, is it?" goes Jen. "You

see, girls, I'm what's known as the brainy one. I wish there was an A-level in Losing It I could take. I could do all the practicals in the science room with a cucumber or something, wearing safety goggles and a lab coat, and not have to do it with an actual *man*. I'd pass with flying colours."

"You'll be fine, when it comes to it," says Lia. "Even I flipped out a bit beforehand. The first time's a big deal. It's only natural."

"But I know I'll just go all awkward when it comes to the real girl-on-guy thing. That's why I wanted it to be with Dylan – he's the only guy I feel comfortable with."

"You'll find The One for you," says Shelley.

I gape at her. I didn't think she believed in love full stop, let alone One True Love. I hope this thing with Stick's not going to turn her into a slush puppy like Jen.

Jen looks thoughtful. "That's what this girl Donna said last night, at the club. . ."

"A lezza?" I go.

"Les*bian*. But how will I find The One for me when Dylan's The One for me? There can't be more than one The One, can there? Isn't that kind of the point?"

Shelley shrugs. "Maybe Donna got it wrong."

"Or maybe it's different for women," I say. "I mean, most women are pretty fab. Maybe lesbians *do* have more than one The One. In fact, I bet everyone does."

Jen groans. "I'm starting to wish I actually *was* a lesbian. Do you know, Donna said I was a hottie? If I was a lesbian I could strut around having my pick of fab women."

"Maybe you could become one," I say, "you know, pledge your allegiance to the furry cup. . ."

"Yuck, what a phrase!" giggles Shel.

"Go on, become a lez, Jen!" I go, trying to make her laugh. "Then we could make out and Jase could video it!"

Jen squeals. "Thanks for the *highly* disturbing offer, Li, but when I think about it there's no va-va-voom. Not even just a tiny va. Which is a shame because girls are great. But guys? Guys like Dylan are hard to find."

"Maybe not," says Shel, "we've both got the guys we want, haven't we, Li? I'm sure there's one for you, too, Jen. How about taking another look at my list, now I don't need it any more?"

"No thanks. Hand me a towel, will you?"

We follow Jen upstairs to her room, where she pulls on black flared slouchy pants and a pink T-shirt that says Angel on it in silver glitter. She sits down at her freaky Iona-shrine dressing table and stares for a moment at that single silver shoe. Like magic, the mirror reflection makes the other half of the pair.

Watching her in the mirror, I see this strange look come into her eyes. "I've got a plan, girls," she says slowly, drawing Iona's tortoiseshell comb methodically through her long black hair. 'Cause it's wet it's all shiny and sleek, like her mum's in the photo. There's something strange in her voice, like she's not really talking to us, but more to her own reflection, as if it's something separate – like a fourth person in the room. It makes me shiver.

"That's the spirit," I go, pretend-jolly, trying to change the atmosphere. "Forget Mr Right, you need Mr Right Now! Let's go and find you some lust object like I've got."

"Oh, no," says Jen slowly, like she's been hypnotized. "It's always been Dylan. It always will be. He's the one I'm going to lose it with."

Jen's reflection smiles approvingly at this, but me and Shel both gape at her.

"Jen, you can't just. . ." Shelley starts to say.

"Why are you always telling me what to do?" Jen snaps, still gazing into the mirror. "Don't you see? It's the perfect way to get over him. You saw how much he cares for me from how worried he was today. It'll just be a friend doing a friend a favour."

"But it won't be that, Jen, will it?" I say. "How can it be when you're completely in love with him?"

"But he doesn't know that, does he?" says Jen, turning to face us at last. "Not unless you told him, *Lia*."

179

She gives me this scary, almost savage, glare.

Normally there's no way I'd let someone talk to me like that. I ought to give her a slap, BFF or not. But for some reason I just shake my head.

"Jen, I don't think this is a good idea," says Shel.

"Well, luckily it doesn't matter what you think," says Jen coldly. "Just because you've managed to get your head out of your backside for long enough to see what's been staring you in the face, doesn't mean you know anything about me and Dylan. But if Stick *does* suddenly announce he's gay and break your heart, then I'll be all ears."

Tears spring into Shelley's eyes, despite the absent look that's come over her face.

We've never seen Jen act this way before. She's never had a go at Shel like that. I mean, fair enough, Shel's a bossy boots – but Jen's well out of order. It's like she's someone else. I can't speak for Shel, but she's scaring the living shite out of *me*.

Shelley stands up and I see her hands are shaking. "Well, we'd better go," she says, fake-cheerful again, just like during the call to Dylan. "Let you get some sleep. If you need me, ring, OK? I'll be at. . ."

"Stick's?" says Jen bitterly. "Yeah, I know." She turns back to the mirror and starts combing the same piece of hair over and over and over.

I just follow Shelley out without saying anything. I don't trust my big mouth.

Outside, though, I explode. "Bloody hell! What's got into her? There's no reason to speak to us like that! We weren't even going to mention our nights, but she wanted to hear! We even had a laugh about it! And then she sort of *turned*. . . It was like she was talking to someone else in that mirror." I don't say *Iona*. Shel doesn't either but I know she gets what I mean.

"Give her time," she says as we get into her car. "She's crashed into reality pretty hard."

"Huh! I'd say she's exited reality altogether! What the hell's this losing it with Dylan idea, anyway?"

"Li, she'll see it's crazy when she's had some rest. She's out of her head with exhaustion. She'll be fine again tomorrow. Let's keep quiet until she mentions it. Otherwise, you know what she's like, we'll just drive her away."

So we don't mention it, not all week. But it isn't exactly hard, because we don't see Jen at all.

16

"Four feet! Omigod, *four feet!*"

Jen hasn't called me or Lia, or come round all week, and we haven't bumped into her in our street. Lia hasn't even seen her at school, now that Mrs Parsons has got this vigilante watch on her going into the sixth form block. We texted Jen this morning to say we were going down to the leisure centre to swim. We don't think she'll turn up, but she does, and she's beaming away like crazy.

"Helloooo!" she cries, virtually skipping in through the changing room door.

"You're back to normal. Thank God," says Lia, never one to beat about the bush.

Jen hugs us both warmly. "Listen, I'm sorry about what I said. I don't know what came over me."

"Forget it," I tell her. "Just as long as you're OK. Have you talked to Dylan?"

"Yeah." She fumbles in her bag.

"Well?" I prompt. "How did it go? Did you tell him how you feel?"

Jen gives me this look like I should be certified

insane. "Of course not! And I'm never going to! Anyway, there's no need. I've got the whole thing into perspective now. It's even kind of funny when I think about it – me going to that club dressed to kill! What on earth was I thinking! Life's too short for moping around. I'm completely over it."

"Good for you," says Lia, patting Jen's shoulder as she squeezes by to go to the loo.

"Oh, Jen," I say. "I'm so glad you've let go of this still sleeping together thing. When you told us about it, I thought it sounded completely crazy. . ."

Jen gives me a puzzled look. "But *that's* not crazy. In fact, it's the only thing that makes any sense. Look, I know it sounds a bit weird, and I don't expect you to understand but, honestly, I'm not in love with him any more."

I stare at her. "Sorry, but I can't believe that. You've been in love with Dylan for ages, Jen. How can you turn off your feelings so quickly?"

Jen gives me this calm smile. "Think how quickly you fell for Stick, even when you thought it could never happen. Falling in love's like that . . . and falling out of love is too."

She's talking as if she's indulging a dim child who just doesn't understand these things. And maybe I am a bit slow when it comes to feelings and stuff. But I'm still not convinced. "But why are you set on sleeping with him? It doesn't make sense."

"It makes *perfect* sense. It's part of the healing process – it's the only way I'll be able to let go properly."

I frown at her. "I don't understand how getting more involved helps you to let go."

"Trust me, I know what I'm doing," she says, inching her costume up under her towel with one hand.

"I wish I could believe that," I mutter.

Lia wanders back over, pulling down the front of her costume a bit to show off her cleavage.

"Jen's still going to have sex with Dylan," I announce, fully expecting her to get on my side, after what she said before, but she just says, "Cool." She's seriously decided to leave Jen to it.

Jen looks at me and raises her eyebrows, like, *see?* I know I should leave it, but there's one thing about this that's really bothering me. The one thing that's strikingly obvious, but Jen doesn't even seem to have considered. "What if he says no?" I say quietly, not looking at her. "You're just going to feel so much worse."

"He won't," she says. Dead certain, just like that. It's spooky, like she's seen the future or something. Knowing Jen, she probably thinks she has. I decide to drop it . . . for now, anyway. "Look, I hope it goes well," I say. "But you will ring if you need us, won't you? If—"

"Thanks," Jen cuts in. "But I won't." Then she does

her famous subject-switching thing and closes the whole topic. "Hey, is Stick coming?"

"God, no! He wouldn't be caught dead in a swimming pool, because that implies doing actual exercise, plus he's pretty shy of his body."

"Stick? Shy?" Lia repeats, incredulous, reminding me how few people see beyond his couldn't-give-a-shit façade.

"Yeah. But he's meeting me down the Lily Pad after."

"How's it going?" Jen asks, as we walk out through the foot baths and into the pool area.

"Really well," I gush. "We get on brilliantly, you know? I mean, we can really talk to each other, and we're into the same things, and we have such a laugh and the physical stuff is great. . ." I trail off. I guess they can tell from my face that something's not quite right, because Jen says, "But?"

I shrug and ease my way down the steps into the pool. It's hard to explain it to them, because I haven't yet been able to explain it to myself. "No, nothing bad. It *is* brilliant and, like I said, we get on really well. It's just. . ."

"What?" Lia says, screwing her face up as she slides into the cool water. They're both looking at me, waiting to understand. Emotion is not my native language.

"Well, I mean, we were going round Sainsbury's the other day, with a trolley and everything, to get some

185

bits for one of his mum's supper parties, and I felt like. . . It felt like. . ."

Jen smiles. "Don't take this the wrong way but you're just flipping out because the biggest commitment you've ever made before is which coat to choose for a season."

I sigh. "Yeah, maybe. And speaking of coats, it's going to be tricky this autumn too, from what I've seen in the shows, with those gorgeous designs from Anna Molinari *and* Marella *and* Aquascutum."

Jen pretends to clear her throat. "Stalling," she hacks.

I give her one of my looks. I found it hard to mention this at all and now she's gone all intense on me. She smiles, *sorry, go on.* "Well, I mean, it feels like Stick's the coat I'll be wearing for the rest of my life."

"But you do still want to rip his clothes off every time you see him, don't you?" That's Lia – of course.

"Yeah, God, *do* I, but. . ."

"Well, there you are then," she says, like that's that, and vanishes. Me and Jen watch her do nearly a length of the pool underwater and pop up near the diving board.

I'm about to follow, when Jen takes hold of my arm. "You're lucky to have it all with Stick," she says, looking really intensely at me. "I mean, the friendship *and* the great sex. People go their whole lives without ever finding someone like that."

Bless her, what a sweetie. "Oh, Jen, you'll get over. . ."

"I know. I *have*. I'm not talking about me specifically, I'm just saying."

I still don't believe her but then I don't seem to have a clue about my own feelings, let alone anyone else's, and it really hit home when she said I'm always telling her what to do. So I decide to shut up and get some exercise.

With all the kids screeching and splashing about I start to wish we'd just gone down to my spa as usual. I'm allowed twelve guest passes a year and so far I've used them all on the girls. But then the reason Lia insisted we come down here walks in with a couple of mates. They're all wearing tight swim shorts and gold chains round their necks. All the twelve-year-old girls start nudging each other and whispering, like some boy band has just turned up or something.

Lia pops back up next to us. "He's here!" she squeals. "Whoor, he's well sexy in those shorts!"

Jase gives her a wave even briefer than his trunks but doesn't come over, even though his mate with the sticky-out ears is checking me out. *Dream on*, I think. Then I remember what Jen said about me being up myself and I give him a quick smile.

Jase dives in and starts doing furious lengths of the pool.

"He'll most likely come over when he's swum a bit," says Lia, sounding disappointed. "Let's do some lengths." She kicks off into some serious swimming then, and me and Jen follow suit.

We stop for a rest about twenty minutes later, panting and bobbing about in the shallow end. Jase isn't pounding up and down any more either, instead he's chatting with his mates by the side. "He's still not taking any notice of me," says Lia, really put out now. "But he bloody well will. I own that guy. Watch this."

She swims over to Jase and gives him a massive snog. Jase looks stunned at first, but soon he's well into it. His mates start off going "whay-hey" and "get in there!" but when it goes on and on, even they get embarrassed and swim away.

"Yuk," says Jen, shuddering. "This has got to be the least romantic place to snog *ever*." The next group due to use the pool is a bunch of old ladies in flowery swimming hats and those sort of Victorian swimsuits that have no danger of showing any pubes. They file in and sit on plastic chairs at the side, waiting for their water aerobics class.

"How are things with your mum at the moment?" asks Jen. She's obviously trying to make conversation to stop me staring at Lia and Jase.

"Pretty good, actually," I say, while still staring. "I've

promised myself I'll try and get on with her better. She was quite motherly when I went on that date with Paul. And she's been so sweet about me and Stick. Maybe we're finally turning a corner."

"Great. I'm really pleased for you."

We watch as Lia slides out of Jase's arms and climbs up the pool steps, very slowly and deliberately. "Where's she going now?" I ask.

Jen shrugs and we swim out a bit and tread water, watching Lia. She smiles at us and heads back through the women's changing room door.

"She must have had enough," says Jen. "The session's nearly over anyway. Oh, look, you can see her feet! That's so cute!"

There's about a three-inch gap all along the bottom of the wall, that you can see through if you're by this edge of the pool. We watch Lia's feet pad into a cubicle.

"Four feet! Omigod, *four feet*!" I squeal.

The two new feet are big and hairy. But what are big, hairy feet doing in the women's changing rooms? We glance around the pool. No Jase. He must have gone out through the men's entrance and then nipped round. "The cheeky sod!" I mutter.

"What on earth are they doing in there?" Jen says.

I give her A Look. "What, do you want me to draw you a diagram?"

Jen's face is a picture of complete disbelief. Then, "Shit!" she says, "lifeguard alert!"

We pretend not to notice the lifeguard watching us and we look everywhere but at the gap. Just to make sure he's properly distracted, I slowly rearrange the top of my swimming costume. Eventually, he tears his eyes away and goes to tell some kids off at the deep end. "Phew, close one!" I whisper. And then we're just staring through the gap and counting feet.

"Four feet."

"Three feet!" I report.

"Three feet? *Jesus!*"

"Four feet again."

"Two swimming costumes!"

"*Two swimming costumes?* No way!"

"Four feet."

"Three feet."

"Two feet."

It's two feet for quite a while after that. Jase's feet.

"Maybe she left," says Jen. "Otherwise why are there only. . ."

"Two feet, two feet, two feet," I go, in time to Jase as he bounces up and down off his heels.

Jen squints at the gap, looking completely scandalized. "No way!"

I turn around and notice Jase's mates standing just behind us, looking right where we're looking, with big grins on their faces. I'm about to distract them, too, when the lifeguard blows the whistle for the end of the session. The session *in* the pool, that is.

But the two feet don't stop moving. In the near-silence that follows the whistle, Lia's voice echoes round the pool. . .

"YESSSSSSSSSSSSSS!"

Lia's in the communal bit of the changing rooms (*sans* Jase) when we get there, sweetly and innocently towelling her hair. She looks up when we walk in and bursts into a beaming smile.

"Lia! We could see your feet!" I whisper.

She giggles. "*Could you?* What a laugh!"

I stare at her. "You don't mind?"

"Nah. We've been seen before anyway."

"*What?*" I say.

"Well, you know that bushy bit in the park where we've been going for all those nature walks? Turns out you *can* see it from the path after all." She explodes into giggles and so do I but Jen looks freaked out.

"Don't you care that people might call you a slag?" she says. "I know that's a real double standard, but things like this get around. You shouldn't have done that today. *We* won't say anything, but his friends saw it too and they're probably right big mouths."

"What do I care? That slag stuff's all a bunch of

hypocritical moralizing crap anyway. I'm going to enjoy myself while I can. We could all get run over by a bus tomorrow."

"I'm totally with you on that, Li," I say. "It's just, we can't help worrying about you. I mean, what if things get serious?"

"Like how?" Lia looks exasperated. "I told you, with me and Jase it's just good dirty fun. It's. . ."

"But what if you fall in love with him?" I blurt out. *Hello*. Where did that come from? I bite my lip but I can't seem to stop talking. "What if it all starts to really matter to you? What if he loses interest or something? Or what if he stays keen and things go well and then you realize that because you love him and you get on like no one else in the universe you might actually never sleep with another man your whole life. And what if you don't want to split up because what if you never find it again, but is that really what you want? No more guys, *ever*? And then what if you start thinking you've got in too deep too soon and you start wishing you'd both let things boil on under the surface for, say, another ten years. But then what if he's with someone else by then so you think you'd better hold on to him and you're happy but it's a desperate kind of happiness that makes you feel like you're drowning and. . ."

I come to an abrupt halt. They know and I know I'm not talking about Lia and Jase.

"That's a lot of *what if*s," says Jen, staring intensely at me.

"Shel, what's up?" says Lia.

I feel really out of control. Panicked. I can't let the girls see that. I take a deep breath and pull it together. "Oh, I don't know. Nothing really. It's just this relationship stuff's all new to me and I didn't realize what a big step I was taking, but I'll handle it. It's fine. Really."

I flip my phone open and glance at the time. "Oh, shit! Gotta go," I say, throwing my stuff into my bag. "I'm meeting Stick at the Lily."

"Give him our love," say the girls together as I head out of the changing room.

"Will do. See yous later."

Love. That's what really matters, isn't it? If I can just keep that in mind, me and Stick'll be fine.

"Shel, what's up?"

I look up and Stick's got this amused little smile on his face. I realize I've been blowing and blowing on my coffee.

"I just want to cool it off a little bit." In my head I pretend I'm saying it about *us*, about the relationship. How would that be? I blow on the coffee again.

"Here, do you want some more milk in it?"

"I'm not talking about the coffee, Stick. I'm talking about *us*."

193

Stick puts down the milk thing and looks at me like I've been struck by some kind of brain fever. Maybe I have. I mean, how the hell did that slip from my mind to my mouth?

"Just a bit. . ." I say weakly. "It's just a bit . . . intense . . . you know."

Stick sits back, looks away. He drums his fingers on the table. "Yeah, sure, if that's how you feel. I don't want to crowd you or anything. I guess we've been hanging out a lot. Nearly every night. We both need time for mates and I've got loads of work to catch up on. . ."

"There's something I want you to know," I say.

I tell him about the date with Paul and how I'd actually planned to lose it with *him* instead. I know, I know. I say Stick must never find out and then I *tell* him? What kind of confessional freak *am* I? Still, at least it's off my chest. Out in the open. Now we can get on with the relationship without. . .

"You didn't have to tell me that," says Stick quietly. "That was before you and me. It's not like cheating or anything. But you knew it would hurt my feelings. You *wanted* to hurt me so I'd back off. You're trying to break us up."

"Stick, I. . ."

"Yeah?"

He looks deep into my eyes and there's this long tense silence that I know I should reach out over. To patch things up. To smile and say I'm being an idiot. Even to blame it on PMS or a row with my mum or that huge bill from the garage. Whatever, to tell him he's got it wrong.

But I don't. Because he's got it right.

Instead I let my eyes blank over and mentally I leave the table and go and hang out by the specials board.

I hear Stick's voice as if from far away. As if he's talking to someone else and I'm just a stranger getting a coffee at the counter, watching from the corner of my eye. "Fine. If you want cool, I'll give you bloody cool. It's over."

Then he gets up and walks out. I don't go after him. I just watch him leave, through my stranger's eyes, from my place by the counter, as if it's nothing to do with me. Then I snap back into myself and get hit by this huge wave of panic.

What about love? How could this happen when we love each other? What's wrong with me? Why couldn't I just be happy being happy? What the hell have I done?

I feel absolutely hideous – lost and confused and torn in half. Tears prickle behind my eyes, although I haven't cried since I skinned my knees at age six. But just when I start to feel like I'm really falling apart, something short circuits in my mind and the wretched feeling vanishes. It's suddenly a huge relief to be alone again. I feel like my old self. I feel safe.

Tony changes the CD to Tom Petty and the Heartbreakers, and when I glare at him he glares back. Him and Stick are really close. In case he hadn't noticed, *Stick* dumped *me*. Well, bollocks to them both.

I tune the music out and decide right here and now, over Stick's cooling cappuccino, to go back to my original plan and give Paul another try. With a defiant glare at Tony I rummage for my mobile and scroll down to Paul's number. OK, so it's not my virginity any more. But that was just the beginning, right? I can still have the fast car and flowers and serious six-pack experience. So what if he's boring – it'll stop me getting involved and messing my head up. I can put this thing with Stick behind me and start again.

Can't I?

17

"We were having a *Volvo*?"

Tuesday night is here at last. I've got Tori's version of that old song "I'm Not in Love" on the stereo, and I'm singing along and staring in the mirror.

Thank God I'm not in love with Dylan any more. Tonight is just about a friend doing a friend a favour. My virginity is one thing I'm not taking back to school after Easter.

"Don't worry, Jenny-bean," says the image in the mirror. "You won't have to. I've always liked that boy. I know it'll work out."

It's really me talking, of course, and not my mum, but it's kind of like I'm channelling her or something. I've got a couple of books about that and some of the stories are really amazing. I've been sitting here quite a lot in the last few days, talking to her and then allowing her to talk back to me. I'm not saying she actually appears or anything, it's just, well, there are lots of things in this world that aren't black and white, that are outside what we can understand. What if, in some magic way, the mirror isn't just a mirror?

What if it's a window?

I put Mum's shoe right up against the glass. The mirror makes a right one to pair up with the left one. I wish I could put on both the real shoe and the reflection shoe and climb into her world – her backwards, opposite world of not-here and not-real, like Alice through the looking glass.

But when I take the left shoe away from the mirror to put it on, the right one disappears. Huh. Deep down I knew it would but for a minute there I'd half thought, maybe this time. . .

The bell rings. Dylan. I go downstairs and open the door to his beautiful smile.

"Hi babe."

We hug hello.

"Hey boy. How's it going?"

"Cool, great, yeah." He hands me a clinking bag from the offie and follows me into the kitchen, peering into the living room on the way. "Nan not around?"

"No, she's still in Brighton with Auntie Rita. You know, sea air and all that." *And it helped that I virtually shoved her on to the coach, too.* "And how's . . . erm. . ." I sooooo want to say *The Blond* in a catty voice. Weird that I still care, but I guess old habits die hard.

"Nick? He's fine. We had a great night last Saturday. . ."

I want to stick my fingers in my ears and go "LA LA

LA LA" but instead I say, "Grrrrrrreat," like Tony the Tiger.

"Yeah. We saw each other Wednesday night as well, at Pete's. Turns out Nick's really into unplugged stuff too."

"Fantaaaa-stic!" I yell. Dylan actually takes a step backwards with surprise, like in those old black and white comedy movies. "You took him to our special place! I'm just so HAPPY!!"

"Me too," says Dylan, giving me a strange look. "Coming out hasn't been half as bad as I thought, actually. Lizzy and Ben said they knew all along, they were just waiting for me to tell them in my own time. I don't know why I didn't do this years ago."

"Me neither," I grump as I unpack a couple of beers and a bottle of red to have now and put the bag in the fridge. I definitely need a drink tonight. I find the corkscrew while Dylan raids the cupboard for Doritos. Then we wander back through the hall and he's about to head into the lounge when I say, "Oh, let's go upstairs. All the good CDs are in my room."

"Sure. I wanted to play you something actually."

We settle down on the rug by my stereo. "So, I didn't get into the boy band."

"Oh, Dylan, I'm sorry. . ."

"Don't be. It was the best thing that could have happened. The guy rang me up afterwards and said it wasn't 'cause I was no good, but that my style was too individual for the group. He reckons I've got the talent to go solo."

"Wow, that's brilliant!"

"Yeah. So I got into the studio at school on Thursday and made a demo. Patrick helped me out a bit. He's taking the Music Tech option. Shall I give it a spin? See what you think?"

"Sure."

He takes a CD out of his coat pocket and puts it into the stereo.

I light some candles and incense as Dylan's voice swells over a lovely bare guitar background, kind of rocky and folky at the same time. I run through a few comparisons in my head – Howie Day, Ben Christophers, Coldplay – but I've never heard anything quite like it. And it's got something like alchemy that makes you just think, *yes*. As soon as I've heard the first track I know he's found his own style.

"It's really . . . wow," I say, lamely, not really able to describe the *something*.

Dylan smiles. "I know I've got a way to go, but it feels right. This is really coming from *me*, you know?"

I nod, 'cause I understand what he's saying, not 'cause I've been there. I'd love to know how that feels – that sense that I'm expressing the true *me*-ness of me.

The other two songs are just as good. The third one's called "Leaving With You" which I listen to really carefully, and enthuse about afterwards, in case he catches on that I used to mind about Nick.

We chat about music for a while, and how Dylan fits in with what's happening at the moment and about his influences. While Dylan goes downstairs to raid the fridge, I pour myself a third glass of wine and make a vow that I'm absolutely going to ask him before the fourth. He comes back with a couple more beers and some mini apple pies courtesy of Mr Kipling. I start telling him about the unis I'm planning to apply to, and what strengths each has, and how I'll probably go to Cambridge if I get in because, well, if you're lucky enough to get a place, you kind of should, shouldn't you?"

"Only if it feels right for you," says Dylan firmly. "It's your life."

I watch him tipping back his head to finish up the beer. There's a confidence, a sort of fluidity he's got now. With the music and coming out he's blossomed somehow. It's like a layer's been scorched away and the *real* Dylan's stepped out of the ashes.

I wish that could happen to me. But then, I'm also scared about what I'd find underneath.

My glass is empty again. So is the bottle, nearly. Well, I may not know who I am, but right now, I know what I want. *Who* I want. And I know I've got to speak now or for ever . . . well . . . or for ever keep my mouth shut, basically. This is it. Time to take a deep breath and a big risk. "Dylan, can I ask you something?"

He smiles at my formality. "Sure."

I go absolutely burning red. I can't believe I'm about to say this. Thank God for alcohol. "I'll understand if you don't want to. It's just, well, the thing is, I'm still a virgin. I really want to lose it but as you know I haven't got a steady boyfriend so. . ."

Dylan grins. "Yeah, sure, Jen. There are a couple of guys at the Brit I reckon you'd like. I could set you up some dates, no problem."

"Actually, I was kind of hoping that you. . ."

Dylan peers at me like he's misunderstood, so I stumble on, feeling more mortified by the second. "Well, that you and me, you know. . ."

The penny drops and so does his face. "Oh! Er, right."

"I mean, you'd be doing me a real favour," I blurt. "Because we're such good friends and. . . I mean, unless The Bl – I mean, Nick, would mind or. . ."

Dylan pulls out his penknife and pings the top off another beer bottle. "Me and Nick aren't exclusive. That's not the thing. The thing is. . . Well, it's just that I don't know if. . . I mean, I've been out with girls before, but that was just playground stuff. I don't know. . ."

He doesn't have to say, *whether I'll be able to get it up*. I get the picture. "Well, could we try? It'd mean a lot. . ."

Dylan looks really torn. I know I should take it back.

His eyes are begging me to say, *hey, never mind, forget it.* Because I don't usually drink I could even blame it on the wine. But instead I let the silence stretch out between us. Then. . .

"OK," says Dylan.

Oh my God, he said yes. He actually said yes! Well, *actually*, he said "OK" but I'm not quibbling.

He gets up, to get a coffee or something, but I don't follow. He turns in the doorway and sees I'm still sitting there, kind of smiling at him. He looks startled. "What, right now?"

"Do you mind? It's just, I've finally got the guts up and. . ."

Dylan leans against the doorframe and sighs heavily. "Are you sure you want it to be this way, Jen?" he asks, looking at his trainers. "I mean, wouldn't you rather wait for someone who. . ."

"No," I say firmly. "I'm sick of thinking about it. I just want the first time over with. And I'd really like it to be with you. If that's OK."

Dylan frowns. "Well, we can try, but sorry if. . ."

"It won't matter."

"Shall I, erm. . ." Dylan makes a motion like pulling his T-shirt off.

I nod. "Yeah, then we could get under the covers."

My hands are trembling as I light some candles and put Nick Drake on the stereo. We get undressed down

to our underwear, not looking at each other, and slide
into my bed.

"This feels weird," I say, giggling despite myself.

"Yeah, for me, too. Should I touch you or. . ."

"It'll be a bit tricky for us to have sex if you don't," I
joke, then immediately wish I hadn't. "Sorry – just
nervous."

Dylan wriggles his arm under my shoulders and pulls
me towards him. He kisses me shyly on the lips, with his
mouth closed. I kiss him back, the same way.

"I love you, Jen."

"I love you too."

We have some more quick little kisses and Dylan
starts easing my knickers down with one hand, his palm
pressing on just the right place, like we've been doing
this for years. A shockwave shoots up my body and I
kind of half-scream.

"Shit, sorry! Did that hurt you?"

"No. Good noise," I say quickly, and so he does it
again, and again. I reach down and take hold of his
penis.

"Sorry, it's. . ." he starts to say.

"It's OK." I move my hand up and down it and he lays
back and closes his eyes and soon it's hard and he's
gasping a little and moving against my rhythm.

My mind's getting shaky. I keep imagining that this is
him and me together – together as in the start of *for
ever*. But I can't slip into that fantasy, or. . .

This is it. I push Dylan's Calvins right down then slide them off with my feet. He moves on top of me, kissing my neck. I can feel him pushed up against me, skin on skin. I'm terrified and excited and . . . oh my God, we are going to do it right now.

It's a huge effort to make myself stop but I manage to say, "Wait. . ."

"It's OK," he says, reaching for his jeans. "I've got some on me."

He pulls an already open packet of condoms from his pocket and shakes one out. I imagine that when he cracked open that packet, he was in some sweaty tussle with my arch nemesis, The Blond. The condoms are called Mates, which suddenly seems like some mystical message about how he feels for me, and how I feel for him. Mates. *Except I don't.*

I'm more in love with him than ever.

I bite my lip but the tears start streaming silently down my cheeks. When Dylan kisses me again he tastes them and rolls off me and holds me tight. "Hey, shush, Jen," he says softly as I sob into his chest. "Is it me? Did I do something wrong? Oh, shit, I knew this was a bad idea."

I shake my head. "It's not you. Well, it is you, but. . . It's. . . The thing is. . ." There's no way round it. It's time to come clean – with myself and with him. If we really are friends I have to be honest with him. I suddenly feel very exposed and pull the duvet up around me. Then I take a deep breath. "I'm in love with you. I have been for years. I thought I was over you, but I've been kidding myself."

Dylan turns and the candlelight flickers off his face. Even with his mouth hanging half open, he looks unspeakably gorgeous. "God, Jen, I had no idea. I thought you knew I was gay. Even before I told you. I mean, it's always been in the air."

"Maybe for you," I say shakily, "but not for me. I've been in love with you since, well, since always. There's never been anyone else. There never *will* be anyone else. And I thought I could still have my perfect first time with you if not the flat and the wedding and the kids and the Volvo and. . ."

"We were having a *Volvo*?" He laughs and shakes his head. "Sorry, but a *Volvo*? Holy shit!"

I giggle too, despite myself. It is kind of funny in a weird, twisted way. "But I realize now it's not going to work," I say. "Doing this won't get you out of my head, it'll just mess me up even more."

"So, you don't want to?"

My stomach knots. *Want to?* Inside I'm screaming for him. For him to hold me and kiss me and make love to me. But I know it's not for real. I tell myself that at least I can get the first time over with, but that doesn't feel like *enough* reason any more.

I shake my head. "Of course I do. But I'd just be pretending it's something it's not. It's time for me to get

206

real." I press my lips tight together, but the tears start sliding down my cheeks again.

Dylan sighs. "Jen, I'm so sorry."

I nod, *I know*. Sorry. That's all he really can say.

We both dress and get back in bed. We lie there in silence, hugging, listening to "Time of No Reply", watching the darkness deepen outside and the candle flames glowing brighter in my room.

We love each other. We're not in love, we're not lovers, but we love each other. And after a while I can't think how anything else could possibly be better than that.

A little later, Dylan falls asleep. Eventually the fire in my body burns itself out, and I drift off too.

I wake up early, slip out of bed and sit in the half-light looking into the mirror. I'm staring, making my eyes go blurry, half-hoping Mum will arrive behind them. But this morning there's just me, and I can't talk to her because Dylan will hear. ! put my fingertips on the mirror and focus on trying to push them through. Nothing happens. I feel a searing surge of disappointment in my chest that I can't reach her. I suddenly have a very clear image of what Dylan would see if he woke up right now. A desperate girl sitting in front of her own reflection in a dressing-table mirror, convinced she's communicating with her dead mother. I shudder.

He'd think I was crazy.

I think he'd be right. I scare myself sometimes. I mean, it's getting so that I *have* to do it early in the morning, otherwise I spend all day thinking about when I'll be able to. It's getting out of hand. Like I said to Dylan last night, it's time for me to get real. The trouble is, I don't feel as if I know what *is* real half the time.

So I wake Dylan up with a mug of tea and a heap of toast, and as we sit there munching I steel myself. I'm not sure how to start so I focus on the detail. As Shelley says, detail doesn't mean trivia. "I nearly got run over after I left Bardot's last Saturday," I say, trying to sound casual. "By a taxi. It was lashing down with rain and it skidded on the road and. . ."

"Shit, I bet you had a shock," Dylan says, spreading another bit of toast with honey. "God, if I'd've known how you felt I'd never have gone off. I should have realized."

I shake my head. "It wasn't your fault. It was mine."

"Don't say that, Jen. It was just an accident."

I put down my mug because my hands have started shaking. "I stepped right out in front of it," I tell him. "It wasn't an accident . . . but I wasn't trying to kill myself either."

"Then what the hell *were* you doing?" I hear the tension in his voice, like he's angry with me for nearly throwing myself away. It shocks me, how fierce he is.

"I guess I was testing fate. Asking whether I'm meant

to be here. Giving the universe a chance to take me, too."

"You mean, as well as Iona?" Dylan grips my shoulder, like he wants to shake some sense into me. "But why would you need to do that, Jen? Of course you're meant to be here."

I feel exasperation welling up inside me, and my words come out all wheezy and strangled. "But I feel like I don't know *how* to be here. I don't know how to be *me*. I'm just acting most of the time in the real world, and I can't find myself inside my head either. I've got this thing with my mirror, like I think she's on the other side of it somehow. I think I can channel her. I feel like I don't know what's real any more."

Dylan breathes out slowly. "Fuck."

"Yeah. Fuck." I stare at the toast, like I've never seen anything so fascinating in my life.

We're silent for a while then, leaning against each other, sipping our tea and watching the sky get lighter. Then Dylan takes my hands in his. He makes me look right into his eyes and, though I try to pull away, he won't let go. I stare defiantly back, even though he's so beautiful I can hardly stand it. He talks slowly and firmly, like I'm still that five-year-old kid in the bathroom. "Jen, there were no fateful forces behind Iona's death. She was out of her head and she was throwing up and she choked on her own vomit. It was a horrible, terrible accident – plain and simple."

"But I can't bear that. If it wasn't fated to be then she just *ended*, for no reason. I'm so scared of it happening to me. Of *ending* one day, just like that. I need to decide *when*. I need to control it."

"Don't talk like that," says Dylan firmly. "It's the same for everyone. We could all suddenly die tomorrow, or live to be a hundred. You can't control it. But that's got to be OK, you know? That's part of being alive."

"But it's too scary. I can't deal with that. I. . ."

"You will," says Dylan, leaning into me. "You will, because you have to. I don't want to sound harsh, Jen, but I think maybe you should see someone about this stuff. A counsellor or something. Like you said, it's time to get real."

18

"Why *can't* I play with your water balloons?"

I'm walking back from the park about half eight (me and Jase were having a little "stroll" in the bushy bit when the ranger came round to lock up and chucked us out). Shame Jase had to go and help Jackie design some new fliers for Brambles. I'm thinking about calling in at Jen's to find out how it went with Dylan last night, but then I remember Shel's mantra – *let her come to us*. We've both been itching to ring her, but Shel's right. So I leave it, even though I'm desperate to know.

I see Paul's silver TT outside Shel's house, so I'd better not call round there either. Funny, I thought they were going to a film. It's a shame about her and Stick. I really thought that was going somewhere. Still, who wants boy stuff to *go somewhere* at our age? I hope they'll get it sorted out and be mates again, though. There was a lot between them. I suppose I could go and do some revision. On the other hand, maybe there'll be something decent on telly. I walk on up the street and I'm just outside *chez moi* when this thing comes flying out of nowhere and absolutely soaks me. I scream. "What the. . .?"

"Ha! Ha! Got you!"

It's bloody Sam, leaning out of the window. I peel the ragged scraps of rubber off my chest. Bloody water balloons – who'd have a younger brother?

But then I realize. Sam hasn't splattered me with a water balloon. He's splattered me with a condom.

Shit! I march into the house and up the stairs, clutching the evidence. I burst into Sam's room and there he is, still leaning out the window with this totally gleeful expression on his face.

"How dare you go into my room," I hiss.

While Sam's mouth is saying, "I didn't," his twinkly blue eyes are saying, *I sure did*.

"Don't lie, you little worm." There's something edgy in my voice that surprises us both. Sam starts bawling on the spot.

So then I've got another problem, how to shut him up before Mum and Dad catch on.

I try to hug him but he leaps back like I'm going to punch him or something. "Why can't I play with your water balloons?" he snivels miserably, from a corner of the room.

And then I realize that's actually what he thinks they're *for*. I catch him into a gentle hug. "Sorry I shouted. There's nothing wrong with playing with my water balloons. But the thing is. . ." I'm thinking on my

212

feet now, "these aren't very good ones. Just give me the packet back and I promise I'll buy you some really brilliant ones in the morning."

Sam looks ruefully at the burst condom in my hand. "But these are great, Lia. They're all slippery and they smell nice like mint."

What the hell am I supposed to say to *that*? *Oh, yeah, Sam, that's so they make blow jobs taste yummy?* I hear footsteps on the stairs. "Give me the packet, Sam," I hiss, through clenched teeth. I don't want to start him off blahhing again, but there's not much time.

"I don't have it," says Sam, launching the last "water balloon" out of the window at a passing pensioner and her dog. "Dad already took it away."

As we both watch the condom splatter on to the pavement below, I kind of wish I could jump out and join it. Because Dad's standing in the doorway, the pack of "water balloons" in one hand and a grim, forced kind of smile on his face.

"Sammy, time to brush your teeth, mate," he says cheerfully. "Oh, and Lia, your mother and I would like a word downstairs, please."

Sam slides off to the bathroom, giving me a baleful look as he passes. I slope down the stairs after Dad and shuffle into the front room.

Mum's sitting on one end of the sofa, bolt upright like she's at a vicar's tea party. She gives me a quick, small smile, like she doesn't want Dad to see her doing it.

Dad. He's pointing at the window. There's something sticking to it.

"Well, at least Sam's aim improved towards the end of the packet," I say, thinking a joke might lighten the atmosphere. "He totally soaked me!"

But I can see from the look on Dad's face that he doesn't see the funny side. "So this is how I find out my daughter's having a *sexual relationship*," he hisses.

"Oh, God, don't say it like that," I say, "like it's something pervy."

"Well? How am I supposed to see it," he bellows, "when I've got to go and peel a burst condom off the living room window?"

"Howie, calm down," says Mum.

I look at her, to smile *thanks*, but she won't meet my eye now.

If this wasn't happening to me it would be hilarious. We'd be creasing up over it in the common room, like we did with that stuff about Carrie and the footprints on the car windscreen. In fact, this is exactly the sort of thing we set up the Goddess Society to avoid.

"Well? Haven't you got anything to say for yourself?" says Dad.

I shrug. "So I'm having sex. Big deal."

Mum starts up now. "But Lia, you're only fifteen.

214

Aside from everything else, it's actually illegal!" She sighs heavily. "I wish you'd at least told us what was going on. I'm really surprised at you."

Here we go. Pack your bags, Lia, you're booked on to the full guilt trip, calling at every station between We Thought We Could Trust You City and You've Really Let Us Down Bay. Toot toot! All aboard.

"I wish I could have told you too," I say acidly. "But I knew exactly what you'd say and I was right."

Mum looks mortified. "Oh, God, I'm sorry, sweetheart. I used to swear I'd never turn into this sort of mum."

We smile at each other, the silly lopsided smile I got from her, and we're just about to go in for the hug when Dad starts on again. He's obviously not ready to get off the anger train just yet.

"Tell me who this boy is," he yells. "It's the one you were canoodling with in the pub that night, isn't it?"

"Canoodling?" I repeat, smirking. I know it's not the ideal time to start wisecracking about his choice of language, but *canoodling*? I just can't help bursting into giggles. It must be the stress.

"It's not funny!" he roars. "It's that Jackie's son, from Brambles, isn't it? How could he be so irresponsible? And you start your GCSEs next month, for God's sake! You should be focussing on that! I'll go down that school and have his guts for garters."

I can't help imagining my dad with Jason's guts wrapped round his legs. It looks so funny it cheers me up quite a bit. Which is probably why I say what I say. Which is definitely a bad idea and responsible for all the shouting that comes next.

"He's not at school. He's not a boy. He's twenty-two."

Dad looks absolutely furious and I start getting scared. He's acting like one of those 1950s deep south fathers who loads up his shotgun and goes screeching off in a pick-up truck and comes back in the middle of the night. You know, where no one says anything about it, even when the police find the boyfriend's body a week later a mile downriver. But I know I'm being ridiculous. My dad's an insurance broker. He's got a Ford Focus and he's never shot a gun in his life.

He's still, erm, apoplectic with rage, I think the phrase is, ranting and raving, so my mum pulls me down on to the sofa and takes my hands in hers. But instead of apologizing again, she says, "Lia, darling, you have to ask yourself why a twenty-two-year-old man is interested in a fifteen-year-old girl."

I stare at her and snatch my hands away. "It's nothing to do with age!" I snarl. "I know what you're implying! Is it so impossible for you to believe that someone could like me for *me*, instead of just wanting to get into my knickers? For your information, I'm fun and clever and he really likes me. How DARE you suggest that. . ."

I fall silent and watch my mum wringing her rejected hands together. She doesn't say it, but it's all there in her face – she may as well be shouting it through a loudhailer: *he's only interested in SEX? That's exactly what I'm saying.*

There's a huge, gaping silence where we all stare at each other. I realize that someone has to do something, and I'm fairly sure I've just said "get into my knickers" in front of my parents, so I reckon it ought to be me. I storm off upstairs and lock myself in the loo. That's when the bad feelings hit me and I can't stand back from them any more. My own father thinks I'm a slapper. My own mother thinks Jase is using me.

I climb into the empty bath, just like I used to when I was a kid pretending to be a rescued turtle, and cry my heart out.

Mum knocks softly on the door, but I call out, "Please . . . I just want to be on my own."

"Look, it's all right, love," she says, through the door. "You *can* talk to us. Even Dad. He doesn't think less of you. He's just worried because he loves you so much. We just don't want you to get hurt."

"I know. . ." I say. "Thanks."

"In a way, we were glad to see the condoms. At least it means you're being responsible!" I raise a tiny snort of laughter. "Well, you just come out when you're ready,

217

darling," says Mum and pads back downstairs. I know it's really truly OK between us, but for some reason, I still can't stop crying. I don't know why I'm like this – it was just a stupid row. Mum and Dad are cool really. I know we can get through anything.

Maybe I'm hormonal with PMS. I work it back in my head – I'm six days late. Yeah, that's bound to be it – I'm coming on.

Or maybe I'm not.

My mind flits back to something I'd almost forgotten about. To the time when we got really carried away and started doing it without a condom. Jase managed to pull out before he came, but. . . I remember freaking out about it afterwards, but Jase promised me it would be OK. He said not to worry. So I didn't.

Oh, God. What if I'm not coming on at all?

19

"How much did I *not* want to see that?"

Paul was meant to be picking me up at home at seven, 'cause he's been making an ad on location somewhere in Kent, but I knew at six there was no way I'd make it back from the studios in time. We still had loads of shots to do. I tried calling him on his mobile as soon as the shoot finished, to say could we meet right at Notting Hill, but he'd got it on message.

That was over an hour ago and he still hasn't got back to me. We'll be too late for the film now. My idea, the cinema — clever, huh? Then we wouldn't have the bother of conversation during the date and there'd be something to talk about in the car on the way to his flat.

But I didn't want to leave more than one message, so after a bit of hanging around, hoping he'd call back, I got in the car to drive home. His job's probably running late too — and you can't have mobiles going off during takes. It's great how we're in the same world — we understand what each other's life is like.

219

Maybe we'll even get together more than once, I'm thinking, driving down Penge High Street, quiet now without its colourful clutter of market stalls. Nearly home. God, I need a shower. Yeah, maybe Paul could be my regular lover boy, no commitment, grabbing time together between work, only when it fitted in. None of the every night stuff I had with. . . I push thoughts of Stick out of my mind. I haven't heard from him since the café episode. I can't believe I just cut off like that – I was so cold to him. I've picked up the phone a few times but never dialled. I wouldn't know how to say sorry – and anyway, he dumped me and bloody well walked out. He's the one who should be apologizing. Oh, God, how stupid to have got involved with a friend. I won't make that mistake again. I guess all I can do now is give it time and hope he doesn't hate me *too* much. When you've screwed up that badly, maybe the best thing is just to draw a line under it and start again with a blank sheet. Maybe even a blank *man*.

I ease up Beckenham High Street in second, rumbling along past the shops. There's one relationship I think I can salvage, though. My mum. OK, so she may not be a domestic goddess like Nigella, but God, Jen doesn't have a mum at all. And when Mum said that thing about being careful when I was going out, it seemed like she really cared about me. We've been getting on so much better recently. Maybe we can leave all that stuff behind and have an adult relationship now.

It's almost nine. Without the date happening me and Mum can maybe stay in together, order a pizza, get a video or something. I nearly pull up outside Blockbuster, but I think, no, shower, get sorted, see what she fancies and then maybe jog down later, get a bit of fresh air.

I turn off Manor Road into our little side street and pull into the drive. I drag my stuff – bag, portfolio, jacket – off the back seat after me, slamming the car door with my hip. I fumble with my keys, fall through the door and, still clutching my stuff, wade straight upstairs to her living room. "Hi, Mum! I'm back! Did Paul come round? Did you tell him sorry I couldn't get him on the mobile. . ."

She's not answering so I pop my head around her bedroom door.

Eeek! *She's in bed with a guy.*

"Oh, sorry!" I start to back away. It's not the first time I've walked in like this.

Then the guy looks up and I can't believe it. It's Paul. I stare. "Oh. He came then," I say acidly.

"Shelley, I. . ."

At least Paul's got the decency to look embarrassed. So he should – she's not exactly fresh goods. I reverse out of the doorway, still clutching my stuff.

"Shel, hang on," says Paul, stumbling up and pulling on his boxers. I don't wait to see if he's going to follow me. I don't want to know. I gallop down the stairs and head out the front door, which I close gently behind me. I'm not going to give her the pleasure of hearing me slam it, of knowing she's got me riled. I notice it now, the Audi parked at the kerb. If Paul'd intended to do this, he'd have hidden it, surely. And as far as I know, they've never met before. She planned it though, I bet. From the second she opened the door and told him I wasn't back yet. *Would you like to come in? Would you like a beer?*

And maybe then he picked up my message, the bastard. He knew I'd be late in.

I could call for Lia or Jen, but I'd rather be on my own for a bit. I told them on the phone about the break up and going for Paul again. They both said I should sort things out with Stick but I did this whole *it's my life and I know what I'm doing* routine and wouldn't have any of it. So I can't face them yet — it's too humiliating. Instead I drive back down the high street, hands shaking on the wheel.

I park up and head into the Slide Bar. Just for half an hour. Just for a couple of drinks to wipe that image out of my head. I sit on one of the vanilla leather and chrome bar stools and order a double vodka and diet Coke. Barmen are more likely to ask me out than ask my age, so there are no problems in that department. I down my drink in about two seconds, get another and sip it more slowly.

I'm mad with Mum, but I'm madder with myself. I should have known she'd do this. Make it into a competition. Is this why I never got involved with any of the blokes before? Was I trying to stay non-threatening to her? I glance at the low faux-suede couches by the big plate-glass window. Couples. Groups. No one I know, luckily. Music starts thumping through the floor and I remember there's salsa in the basement tonight. Hoo-bloody-ray.

Where's Oprah when you need her? Well it's sorted one thing out, anyway. That's the end of me and Paul. There's no way I'm going where she's been. She knew that too. I bet she loved the look on my face. Loved proving she's still got it. Bitch.

A bloke comes over and offers to buy me a drink but I say no thanks. Right now I'd rather be on my own, however sad I look. I get another double myself. And another.

I'm gazing blearily through the window when a face in a crowd going by makes me focus.

It's Stick.

Bloody typical. I'm miserable, alone, half-cut and badly in need of a shower and hair wash. When he next saw me, I was supposed to be deliriously happy, surrounded by mates and looking and feeling like I'd just stepped off the cover of *Zest*. "Please don't come in, please don't come in," I mumble into my drink.

Stick comes in with a rabble of expensively

underdressed mates from school, and a few St Mary's girls. His arm's slung casually round the shoulders of one of them – she's small, neat, really classically pretty, not strange-looking and gawky like me. *You didn't waste any time*, I think sourly. But then, I guess I didn't either.

Stick spots me and comes up to the bar. He says *hi* uncertainly, and I say it back. I think that might be it, but he stands beside my stool as he gets a round in. So I reckon it's OK to make conversation. "Well look at that," I say. "You've got yourself a real live girl there. 100% not pretend."

Stick half-laughs. "She's Alicia's sister, back from Leeds Uni." He's not looking at me – focussing instead on loading pints on to the tray the barman's just handed him. "She's seeing someone up there. I'm just enjoying the glow 'cause I know she fancies me. I'll probably shag her later, give myself an ego boost."

I laugh a bit too hard.

Stick looks flustered. I realize that he doesn't want me to see through him any more. I'm supposed to buy his blah the way everyone else does. So that's what I pretend to do. "Why do you need an ego boost?"

Stick shrugs. "Oh, my bitch girlfriend screwed me over."

"Huh. What a coincidence. My bastard boyfriend dumped me."

"Touché."

We smile at each other. Not exactly forgiven, but. . .

Stick takes the tray over to the table and unloads. He comes back with it, hands it over to the barman. I think he's going but then he says, "Do you want to. . .?" He gestures at the table.

"No. Cheers, but I'm not feeling so sociable right now."

"What *are* you doing in here then?"

"Getting hammered. How about you?"

"We just came in for a quick one before heading down to the indie double bill at the Studio, but hammered sounds appealing. I think I'll hang back for a bit, if you don't mind."

I shrug. "Sure. I'll probably pass out at about ten fifteen, so you'll make the second movie . . . and still have time to shag the sister."

Stick gives me a look, not sure whether that was a piss-take or a peace offering. "We'll see," he says.

He has his drink with his mates, then peels away when they head for the door and takes the empty bar stool next to mine.

"You know the best way to get really drunk and also exercise?" I say. "Tequila slammers. All that banging on the table's wonderful for muscle tone."

So that's what we do. Get hammered on slammers. Slammered, ha ha. I lose count of the times the barman lines them up and we lick, bang, drink, bite.

"So why are you here on your own?" says Stick, between rounds.

"Oh, you know what you said about getting an ego boost?" I slur. "Well, my ego boost went tits up." I tell him about Paul and my mother. Needless to say, only the essential details. Sadly, the tequila haze hasn't made it any less horrendous. "I mean, her and Paul – eww! – how much did I *not* want to see that?"

"I'm thinking, very much with the not seeing," says Stick. His grammar's obviously gone to Mexico. *Lick, bang, drink, bite.*

"I mean, how could she do that to me? I realize how fucked up she is now, how fucked up she's always been. I thought we were finally getting somewhere, too. Well, she can't mess with me like this. I've got enough money saved for a deposit on my own place. Soon as I find somewhere, I'm out of there. That's what she's wanted since I was about fourteen anyway."

"Yeah, good for you, Shel."

"Yeah, good for me."

"Yeah." And he bursts out laughing. That's when I realize how funny it is. Gross, and yukky and twisted, but very very funny.

"I have to leave home," I say, "because I can't trust my mother not to seduce my dates."

We laugh for a long time, but then I stop suddenly, 'cause there's something I've just *got* to say. "I can't believe you walked away, Stick."

The laughter drops from his eyes. "I can't believe you let me."

"I know."

"I wanted you to follow me. All you had to do was get up and follow me." Stick puts his fingers on the bar and does an impression of one little person running after another. He looks up at me, red-eyed. "Just like that."

I watch the finger people running across the bar. While I'm grateful for the diagrams at this stage, it's no use pretending this is news. "I know," I say. "I wanted you to go."

"Ouch," says Stick.

But I don't want him getting the wrong idea, so I decide, or rather the tequila decides for me, to come clean about what happened in the café. "Not because it wasn't working. But because it was. It scared me. I was scared of it going on working and that being *it* for the rest of my life. It all happened so quick – first we slept together and then suddenly I was your girlfriend. . ."

"But you said—"

"I know. I wanted to be. But then Jen made me realize I was in love with you and it all started getting. . ."

Stick stares at me and I clamp my hand over my mouth, although it's far too late to take it back.

"You were in love with me?"

I wrinkle my nose up, embarrassed. "*Yeah*. And then

there was Sainsbury's and well, the point is, it started freaking me out."

"You were in love with me," repeats Stick, sounding amazed.

"Shut up, already," I squeal, cringing. I take a deep breath. "OK, so I was. But, being that close to you, I felt like I was losing myself. I didn't know how to handle it."

Stick laughs bitterly. "Crazy, isn't it? You loved me. I loved you." I shiver when he says this. I thought, maybe, but it's different to actually *hear* it. "I am the bloody Love Magician," he says. "I fix people's relationships. That's what I *do*. But ours doesn't work 'cause it's too *good*? That's insane!"

"Crazy." I snigger and soon we're both snorting with laughter again.

"Crazy, crazy, crazy," mutters Stick, tilting the bar stool so far back it nearly goes over.

I grab for him and when he's upright again I don't let go of his arm. It's suddenly all become startlingly clear. I know what I want. And for some reason, it doesn't scare me any more. "We'll make it work," I say. "I get it now. This is so much better than anything else. I want you back, Stick." I lean forward and kiss him, tasting the lemon and salt on his lips. He kisses me back, hard and deep.

The bar suddenly seems far too public a place for our great reunion.

"Come on, let's go back to yours," I whisper, though how I feel at the moment, I'd settle for sneaking him into the ladies' loo, or driving up to the woods and fucking him on the back seat of my car.

I take his hand and try pulling him off his stool but. . .

"No, Shel," he groans, "this very bad idea. You were right. We're too young. You'll always be wondering about other guys. And if I'm honest, so will I. Not about *guys*, obviously, but. . ."

"I don't care about that any more."

"But you will. I don't want to take that away from you."

"But I *want* you."

"Exactly. You *want* me. But what about when you don't any more? I can't deal with you changing your mind again." Stick swallows a shot of tequila straight, like it's medicine. "I mean, you just switched straight off Paul, on to me, then off me on to him. You'd probably be there now if things hadn't gone so horribly horribly."

I'm close to tears now. Why won't he understand? "I know that's how it looks but really, it's not." *Please, Stick, just shut up and take me home and. . .*

"Face it, Shel, you would."

I realize that Mum's done me a huge favour, because now I know what I want. I'm not going to lose him again. "Before, yeah. But not now. . ." I lean forward to kiss him, but he tips his stool away. "Sorry, Shel."

I don't even rummage for a tissue. I just let the tears make trails down my cheeks. Stick looks shocked to see them, then pained that he's making me cry them. When I speak, they run into my mouth. "Can't we at least keep sleeping together?"

"You know we can't. It can't be casual with me and you."

I get a head rush at the memory of sex with Stick. Then I think about it never happening again. "Please don't do this to me."

He sighs. "Look, we're so lucky we've made it through this still talking. And I'm glad we did get together. I can't think of a better way to have lost it than with you. But really, Shel, I'm saying no."

I blink at him. That's *it*? I almost can't take it in.

This is my cue to say, *fine, sod you then*, and switch off, but I can't seem to detach. Instead I feel the full force of rejection like a punch in the stomach.

Stick pulls me off the stool. "Come on, I'll get you a cab."

"I can drive."

"No way."

"*Yes* way. Look, I'll do the straight-line cop test." I stand up, take a couple of steps and nearly fall over. Stick grabs me and pulls me upright.

I stare into his eyes and will him to kiss me. He looks away. "But I *always* get what I want," I whisper.

"Not this time," mutters Stick. "Really. I just want to be friends, OK?"

"I don't know if I can do that," I say. And it's true. I don't know if I can bear it, being around him and not being with him.

"Come on." Stick grabs my elbow and steers me out of the bar.

And even though we're both off our heads, I know he's serious.

20

"Where are the goddesses now?"

The doorbell goes about half eleven, and I creep downstairs to answer it with a big block of rose quartz in my hand. I once heard a horrible story about some rapist who just rang this girl's bell and then when she opened the door, he forced his way in and attacked her.

I look through the little square of glass and put my weapon down – it's Shelley. She's leaning limply against the porch, black mascara tears running down her face.

"God, what happened to you?" I ask, pulling her into a hug and grimacing at the stink of spirits on her breath.

"He loved me," she slurs. "He said that, you know? He loved me and I loved him and I messed it up. Bad. Irrep-prebably."

I drag her into the kitchen and prop her against the counter. This looks like a job for strong black coffee. "Who loves you? Paul?"

She gives me a withering look.

"*What?*" I cry, waving a teaspoon. "His car's been outside your house all evening. I assumed. . ."

"Stick."

"*Oh.* But if you were out with Stick, what was Paul's car doing. . ."

Shelley stares intensely at me. At first I don't believe she can possibly mean what I think she means. But she doesn't stop doing the stare, so I say, "Not your mum. . ."

She nods.

Ew! She must be so embarrassed. I don't want to make it worse, so I try to act like it's a normal thing that happens all the time. "Stupid cow. Look, come upstairs and you can tell me about it, OK?"

Shelley nods and sniffles. "He loved me. He said so," she mutters forlornly as she shuffles up the stairs.

I follow her, nearly slopping the coffee over myself as she sways backwards. In my room she collapses on to my purple velvet bedspread. I nearly ask her to sit on the floor, 'cause I don't want her perfume erasing Dylan's smell, but I bite my tongue. I haven't even pulled the covers straight since he left this morning – it's like the bed's become a work of art I've got to preserve. How sad am *I*? I put the coffee on top of the CD player and turn the volume down low. "Start at the beginning," I tell her.

Shelley hauls herself upright. "He loved me. He

loved me and I wrecked it." She mimes driving a car into a wall. "Boom! Wrecked! He loved me. Did I mention that?"

"Once or twice," I murmur, handing her the coffee. I know she's off her head, but I hadn't realized quite how badly. I pull a few balled-up tissues out of my bin and put it next to the bed. Just in case. "So what happened?"

"Came home late. Live sex show in Mum's bedroom. Went to the Slide Bar. Had a couple of drinks. Stick came in. Couple more drinks. I tried to make up with him, but he wouldn't have it. Mates, he said. No relationship. No sex even. Well, big hairy pants to *that*."

Bloody hell. "Oh, Shelley, I'm so sorry."

She shrugs, gulping at the coffee although it must still be too hot.

"If it's any consolation, I had a Mates Moment, too," I say, "so I know just how you feel. Dylan came over last night and I realized I'm still in love with him. It all came out in the end. We didn't do it."

Shelley looks at me and her eyes fill up with tears again. I've never seen her cry before, but now she can't seem to stop. "Oh, lovely, lovely Jen," she mumbles. "That's shit."

Then she leans forward, puts the mug down and grabs her head in her hands. "Whoa!"

I hold my bin out for her but she waves it away. "Nooooo. Too gross to clean. I can make the bathroom." She half staggers, half trips down the narrow stairs. I follow close behind. She lurches for the loo and pukes half in it and half round it. She keeps hurling again and again, convulsing and retching. It's horrible, like she's going to throw up her insides.

Eventually she stops, leans her head against the toilet rim and goes very limp, very still, very silent.

Suddenly this black terror slithers up my body like a snake, drawn by the acrid smell, that mix of perfume and spirits and vomit. I start screaming, but it sounds far away, like someone else. I watch my fingers grab one of her silver sandals and fumble desperately with the buckle.

She comes to life and shakes me. "Jen! Jen, calm down! I'm fine! It's OK!"

But I can't stop screaming and my fingers won't stop scrabbling with the sandal. That slender foot. Those silver toenails. Painted to match, of course. I always take her sandals off – first thing I do when she gets in the door. She always sighs with relief when I unbuckle them, like they're a corset, slow-choking her. If I can just get them off, then she'll breathe. If I can just get them off, then she'll *live*.

It's only when Shelley slaps me that I drop her foot and fall silent. I stare at her, bewildered.

"Sorry, I had to do that," she whispers, hugging me.

"Christ! I thought you were. . ."

"Iona. I know."

I lean up against the bath. Shelley doesn't look half so pissed any more. Maybe the chucking up brought her round. That or the shock. Now she just looks pale and terribly frightened. I wonder why and then I realize – she's frightened of *me*.

"It's all starting to come back," I say. I'm trying to sound as normal as possible but Shelley still looks wary. "I know why I've got the shoe. She was throwing up like that, like you, and then she started jerking even worse and went this horrible colour. I didn't know what to do. It seemed to go on for ever. I forgot all that stuff she'd taught me about taking the emergency money from her top drawer and running to the phone box on the corner of Darville Road to call 999. I just forgot it all – I didn't know what to do."

"You were five, you couldn't know," says Shelley softly, the fear gone from her eyes.

Now the memory comes fully alive and the story surges inside me, gathering pressure where it's been interrupted. My voice is flat, steady. I'm not really talking to Shelley, or even to myself. I'm just talking. "Then she fell back on to the floor – it was chunky old quarry tiles, I can see them now. Her eyes were open but she wasn't *in* there and I didn't know what to do. I peed all down my legs, just kind of standing there, begging her to stop it. Then I remembered about the emergency money but it was dark outside. I was too scared to run to the phone box. It sounds crazy, but I didn't really even know if it was an emergency. I didn't want to get in trouble for spending the money if it wasn't. We had to be ever so careful."

"Of course," says Shelley gently.

"I got one shoe off and hid it in my toy box. I tried to get the second one off, but her foot was heavy on top of the strap. I couldn't do it. I thought that if only I could, she'd come back. She used to always say her shoes were killing her, and play being in agony, and I used to love to take them off for her, quickly, you know, so I thought. . . But I couldn't do it. Her leg was just so heavy and I couldn't turn her.

"Then I remembered Lizzy and Ben, Dylan's mum and dad. They'd be able to get the strap undone. I ran down the hall and the stairs and thumped on their door. When I explained what I needed help with, they told me to stay with Dylan and went tearing up to our flat. Ben must have run down to the phone box then, because I heard him on the stairs and the slam of the front door. I remember hoping he'd use his own emergency money. I kept trying to wake Dylan up but he was too sleepy, so in the end I just lay there hugging him, watching the blue lights sweep patterns across the room and listening to footsteps on the stairs, crackling walkie-talkies, doors opening and shutting."

I touch my face and realize I'm crying. But it's just water pouring. It hardly shows in my voice. Now that

I've started, there's no way I can stop. Not for tears. Not for anything.

"Lizzy went in the ambulance. I stayed behind with Ben and Dylan. No one told me what was happening, and I didn't know how to ask, but Ben came and sat on the bed. He woke Dylan up and pulled us both into his arms and we all just sat there all night, till Lizzy came back when it was just getting light. I remember she made us this lumpy porridge and I asked her if she had any cocoa powder because my mum usually put it in so it went chocolate. She looked at me and burst into tears. Funny, she never told me that bit."

I lapse into silent staring then and Shelley strokes my arm. "Is that all you remember?"

"I think so." Then I sit bolt upright as a new episode explodes into colour in my mind. "Oh my God. A man came and took lots of our things. Some of the neighbours made rude comments and Lizzy spat at him." I look her straight in the eye. "What if it was my dad?"

She takes a deep breath. "Jen, you can't make assumptions. It could have been the landlord. Maybe your mum owed money."

"Maybe. But what if it was *him*? If it was he took nearly everything except me."

"Jen, it could have been anyone," Shelley insists. "A friend, a lover, some debt-collecting guy. And even if it *was* your dad, that just shows what a rat he was, doesn't it? Look what you've got with your nan. If your dad had claimed you, Social Services might never have got in touch with her."

"Yeah, I suppose." I don't want to drop it, but Shelley's right. How can I know, and even if I did, what could I do about it? I fish for more memories, but there's nothing else. "So then Nan came, and we moved here," I report. "And that's it." I feel weightless and empty and strangely peaceful. I've finally got the whole story, and it was inside me all along.

"But now you've got to get on with your life," says Shelley firmly. "Iona's gone."

"I know. I mean, *really*. I just wish I knew *where*."

Shelley looks really intensely at me, like I've suddenly turned into a complete stranger. "But I thought you'd found something to believe in?"

Something to believe in. I've tried on almost every idea, from reincarnation to heaven to universal energy to simple soulless worm food. I have a feel for the new age metaphysical stuff, but there's this voice in the back of my head always wondering if it's just a comfort. In the end I'd rather have hard truths than easy lies. But I *can't* have truth, can I? Only belief. "Why isn't belief enough for me?" I ask her. "It seems to work for other people."

Shelley sighs. "I don't know, Jen. I really don't know."

Just then the doorbell rings again. I go down and

239

grab the rose quartz, but it's only Lia. She looks questioningly at my bloated red eyes but I don't say anything apart from hi. Instead I just walk into the kitchen and put the kettle on again. "So what's up?" I ask finally.

Lia shrugs. "I don't need a reason to come round, do I? Just thought you might like to see me."

I give her a funny look. What a strange thing to say. "Course. I always like to see you," I tell her. "It's just, it's pretty late." I put out three mugs and spoon instant coffee into them. Maybe I'll even get to drink it this time.

Lia clocks the mugs. "Oh, God, sorry, Jen. Is Dylan here? I'll go. . ."

I shake my head. "Shelley," I say. "Very drunk, except she's thrown up now so she's a bit better."

Lia frowns. "But what about Paul? I saw his car outside her house earlier. I thought they were going to the cinema."

I explain about Paul and Di, and Shelley's Great Realization about Stick and how he blew her off in the bar.

"Bloody hell!" Lia takes her mug and follows me up. We pass the bathroom and I see that while I've been downstairs, Shelley's cleaned up and put the bleach round. A bit haphazardly, but thank God *I* didn't have to do it.

We get up to my room and find her propped up on

cushions on my bed. Me and Lia join her and I realize I'm not thinking of it as defiling the sacred Dylan bedspread any more.

"Lia, hi," says Shelley, taking the steaming mug from me. "How did you know I was here?"

"I didn't. I just came over. But I'm glad you are."

"You won't get much entertainment out of us," Shelley tells her. "I've had the evening from hell."

Lia sips at her coffee. "Jen said. Sorry about that."

Shelley sighs and burps tequila. "He loved me, did she tell you that? And did she say that *she*. . ." Shelley points at me like Lia won't know who she means otherwise, ". . .that *she* just had this totally spooky flashback to *you know when*?"

Lia blinks at me, but I don't want to talk about it, so I say, "Come on, Li, cheer us up with some gossip about your straightforward, no strings lust-life. How's it going?"

Lia sips at the coffee again. "Oh, fine, yeah. Brill. Except I think I'm pregnant."

I almost drop my mug. I mean, Christ! People should flag up when they're going to say something like that.

"Have you done a test?" says Shel, sitting bolt upright.

"No, I only just realized I'm late. I had this stupid row with Mum and Dad 'cause Sam was using my condoms as water balloons and. . ."

241

Shelley snorts with laughter and then mumbles, "Sorry. Inappropriate Girl strikes again. I'm still quite pissed over here. Carry on."

"It's OK. It was pretty funny. Dad nearly burst a blood vessel. I sat in the bath for ages crying for no reason and then it dawned on me – six days late. There was this one time in the park when we got carried away and didn't use a condom. Jase pulled out but there was this little bit of stuff but he promised it would be OK and. . ." She starts crying then, fat tears plopping into her coffee.

We both lunge over and hug her. God, I could *kill* Jase. I knew it. I just knew he was trouble. The cards never lie. But I know that's not what Lia needs to hear right now. "Shush. You don't know yet. Let's not jump the gun."

"But what if I am?" she wails. "I can't ask Jase to give up his freedom just like that, but he's bound to want to look after us. We'll have to get a flat and I don't know how to do any of the housework stuff his mum does for him, like ironing and that."

Me and Shelley just stare at each other over her head. What is she, crazy? Worrying about Jase's ironing at a time like this?

"We'll get a test first thing in the morning," I say. "Then we'll know."

Lia smiles wanly. "Thanks, you guys. But I think I'd better do it with Jase. After all, we could be talking about our baby here. If it's positive, he'll want to be there, won't he?"

Shelley explodes, spitting half her coffee back in the cup. "Lia, you're not talking about keeping it, surely? This isn't 'Papa Don't Preach'! It would be for the rest of your life. You do realize you're *fifteen*, don't you? I mean, haven't you *read* the *Megan* books?"

"Yeah, course, but it's made to look harder in a book, isn't it, to make it more exciting. It wouldn't be so bad in real life. And in *Megan* the dad didn't help out, but Jase would."

I wouldn't be as quick as Shelley to suggest abortion. I'm not sure it's right. Still, even I can see that Lia's in la la land. I've got to wake her up. "*Hello? Jase take responsibility? Are you completely crazy?*"

"No, I'm just bloody terrified," she snaps. "I mean, what if I really am pregnant? What will Mum and Dad say? What the hell will I do about my exams? They might kick me out of school and. . ."

Usually Shelley bangs our heads together when we start fighting like this, but she seems to have passed out, so I guess we're going to have to sort this one out ourselves. I take Lia's hand. "Calm down," I say gently. "There's no point getting in a state. Look, that chemist in Village Way opens at seven. We'll get the stuff first thing and do a test. But till then, try not to panic. You don't know for sure yet. Chances are it's a false alarm."

"Yeah, you're right," says Lia, sighing deeply.

"Thanks. Look, let's try and talk about something else. How did it go with Dylan?"

"It didn't," I say flatly. "I'm still in love with him and I ended up telling him so and then I couldn't go through with it."

Lia's face drops. "That's shit."

I can't help smiling even though I feel terrible. "That's exactly what Shelley said. But look, it's OK. Dylan's just been part of it. I've been going off my head a bit with this stuff about Mum. I mean, I haven't been sure whether I want to be here."

Lia looks questioningly at me. "I don't get what you mean."

"You know. Here, capital H. On this physical level of existence."

Lia looks startled. "But, Jen, of course you should be here. You belong here, 'on this physical level of existence', as you put it, with us. And, anyway, what if there *are* no other levels of existence? What if this is it? You'd be screwed then, wouldn't you?"

Normally I'd never laugh at something like that, but the way she says it makes me smile despite myself. She smiles at me smiling. "Come on, Jen. Can't you just focus on what's here in front of you?"

I nod. "I know that's what I need to do." I didn't think Lia would be much help with this, but actually she really is, so I tell her how I've been feeling. "Half of me *does* want to be here. But it's as if the other half of me

244

already went with Mum. I feel like half of a pair but I can't find her, no matter where I look. I try to be like her, but I don't sparkle – not like she did. Remember last year, when I spent Nan's birthday money on that coral-coloured beaded cardigan in the Monsoon sale? It was hand wash only and I didn't know when I'd wear it but it was the sort of thing Mum would have loved. I just wanted that moment when Nan said, *oh Jen, you look just like Iona*. For one moment I wanted to give her her daughter back."

"You can't be her, Jen. You've got to be you."

"But I don't know *how*."

Lia glances towards the dressing table. "Well, you could start by putting that creepy stuff away." She looks down as soon as she's said it. I can tell she thinks I'm going to get mad with her. I would have done before now. But it's as if reliving the story shifted something. I know she's right.

"Good idea," I say. "It'll help me let go of Dylan too. I think I've been clinging to this idea about us because I couldn't stand the thought of being with someone she didn't know. But I can't have him, however much I'm in love with him. It's just not going to happen. This gay thing isn't just a phase. I understand that now."

"But with me and Stick it could have worked out," wails Shelley, suddenly coming round. "I had the chance you didn't and I blew it! I'm such an idiot! He loved me, did I tell you that?"

"Just a few times," I say, breathing deeply, not knowing whether to laugh or cry. "Anyway, how do you know what we've been saying? You were passed out."

She winks at me – she was awake all the time, she'd just decided to let me and Lia talk a bit, the sly thing.

"But he doesn't want me now!" she wails. "He doesn't trust me after I went running back to Paul. And I loved him too. I still do. Did I say that?"

"Uh-huh," says Lia, catching on to the not-funny joke.

We all start laughing and crying at once. If there's a word for that I don't know it.

"We were supposed to be having fun, losing our virginity," Shelley sobs and giggles. "That's what the Goddess Society was for. Why did falling in love have to come into it?"

"Why did falling in love have to *not* come into it, you mean!" I wail.

"Bollocks to all this love stuff," gasps Lia. "I mean, *hello*! I've got an actual real problem here. Why did no one mention how easy it is to get pregnant?"

It's so not funny, but it so is. Maybe this is what hysterical means.

"Where are the goddesses now?" Shelley asks me, as if I thought up the whole thing not her and this is all my fault. "All I see are three bloody miserable mortals."

"It's nothing to do with the Goddess Society," I say. "Everyone loses it. Everyone gets involved. It stands to reason everyone must get hurt as well, some of the time."

We all go silent then. We hadn't noticed the stereo playing. It's been quietly working it's way through the five CD changer unheard. But we listen now. As usual at mine, Tori's singing.

"Girls, you've got to know when it's time to turn the page.
When you're only wet because of the rain."

Now the crazy laughter stops and we just cry – for ourselves and for each other, for fear of what's ahead and for grief at what we've left behind.

21

"...in a non-sexual way, obviously."

We sleep in our clothes, all jumbled up on Jen's bed. I wake up early and slip downstairs to make myself a cup of tea. I sit at the kitchen table, sipping the tea, and then rummage in Jen's handbag for some tablets, to try and shake the headache I've got from crying so much last night. The packet reads: *Caution: if pregnant consult your doctor before taking.*

I jump. I'd got hazy about this, and it's suddenly real again. I was hoping I'd come on in the night, but still nothing. I take the tablets anyway, as if what I don't know can't hurt me. I want a bit of time on my own before I do the test, before I call Jase even. That's a first – I've never wanted time on my own before. I just sit, imagining how it might be if I am. Me carrying the baby in one of those things you strap to your front. Me getting baby food in Sainsbury's. Mum helping me pick out the right stuff in Mothercare, telling me to get plain white babygros that can easily be thrown in the wash and frowning if I choose anything denim. I remember some of it from when Sam was born, but mainly I just remember being furious because he'd arrived two days before my seventh birthday and completely hijacked it. Mum and Dad weren't up to doing me a proper party and he got loads of presents and attention. For about three months after I had this master plan to sneak into their room, lift him out of his cot and put him back where he came from. Luckily for Mum I never tried it.

God, sitting right here now, *I* could be a mum, and I don't even know it. I could have a baby marinating inside me. It could be in there *growing* right now. That freaks me out so much I bolt upstairs again.

"I'm going to call Jase," I say, shaking Jen and Shel awake. They both look like death and I realize I must too. Neither of them say, *but it's 6.30*, or, *leave us alone we've only had four hours' kip*. They're good mates, these two.

Jen hands me the pink bakelite phone by her bedside. "Do you know the number?"

"Yeah, off by heart." I dial slowly, hands shaking. I always call his mobile, 'cause he says Jackie gets funny about him tying up the house line, and anyway it's 6.30 a.m. Shel and Jen scoot up next to me on the bed, one each side. I hit the last digit. I could be about to change Jase's life for ever.

I nearly lose my nerve and put the phone down after four rings. But then he answers, in a gruff morning voice. "Ye-lo?"

My heart's pounding in my ears. I wonder if he can hear it. "It's Lia."

"Lia? It's bloody early to be. . ."

He's whispering. "Why are you whispering?"

"I'm not, am I? Look, I can't talk now. I feel too rough. I've got flu or something."

"Sorry, it's just. . ." I was going to make some small talk first, but I realize now I have to come right out with it or he'll hang up. "I think I'm pregnant."

Silence. Then he says something I never would have expected. He says, "Ha ha, very funny. Now, go back to bed and I'll ring you later, OK?"

How could he think I'd find that funny? What sort of idiot does he think I am? "I'm serious, Jase."

More silence. Then, "But we've always been. . ."

"Careful, yeah, but there was that one time, remember? In the park? And I was freaking out, but you said. . ."

"But you can't be. We were just having a laugh."

That pisses me off – course we *were* just having a laugh, but we're obviously not *now*, are we? "Oh right, thank goodness for that," I snap. "I'll just explain that to the baby, *sorry, we were just having a laugh*, and it'll disappear. Thanks so much, Jase."

"I only meant. . . Look, if you are, just get it sorted, OK? Pronto. They'll do one no questions, 'cause of your age."

I can't believe he's being so casual about it. And so

sure, like it's obvious what I should do. "We're supposed to decide that together," I say.

"I don't want a kid now."

I can't believe it. He's acting like the guy in those crap sex education videos we watched at school. I thought they were so funny at the time.

Then I hear a sleepy mumble in the background. A *voice*. "Who is it, Jase?"

Female. *Hazel*.

I stare at Jen and then at Shel, but their expressions haven't changed. They obviously didn't catch that. Now there's rustling. Jase must think he's covered the receiver, but he hasn't – not quite. I hear him say, "No one. Go back to sleep."

I should be furious, but I don't have the energy. I suddenly feel far older than fifteen, and completely exhausted.

"Lia? Are you there?"

I slowly put the phone down. The girls are staring at me, and I realize I should probably say something.

"He's got a girl there. His ex. He said I was no one." I report this like the weather. Why can't I get angry?

Jen winces.

"The bastard!" says Shel, absolutely spitting bricks. "What a wanker!"

Hearing her get so mad helps me dredge up a bit of

annoyance. "Yeah. Flu my ass. He must have gone to the pub after I went home and had a few drinks and got off with Hazel. On the same *day*. Probably hadn't even had a shower. That's so rough."

"Sod him," says Shelley firmly.

"I can't just. . . He could be the father of my child." It sounds unreal, like something out of a film.

"Sod. Him." Clearly, Jen's with Shel on this one.

"Steady on," I tell her. "Where's your compassion and all that spiritual stuff gone? We're talking about my baby's father here."

"Maybe," says Shel, all thin-lipped. "We'll see. Listen, put the kettle on. I'll nip back and get my car and then drive to that chemist in Village Way, get some tests." And she pulls her boots on and storms out the door in a crumpled whirl of stale alcohol.

Jen makes some tea and I drink it down fast and have a second cup. I'm about to go to the loo but she says, "Save it. You have to wee on the stick."

Shelley comes back and gulps down her half-cold tea as we go up the stairs and file into the bathroom. She hands me a paper bag with three packets in. "Just how pregnant do you think I am?" I joke. Soooo not funny.

"In case it doesn't work," says Shel.

"Do you want us to wait outside?" asks Jen.

My legs are trembling so much I have to sit down on the loo seat. "No, please stay. OK, here goes."

I lift the seat and take the test out of the packet. Then I pull my jeans and pants down and sort of crouch over the loo.

Nothing happens.

"What's the matter?" asks Jen.

"I can't do it. 'Cause you're looking."

"We'll go," says Jen. "We'll just be outside the door."

How can I explain how much I need them in here? "Stay, please. Just, like, close your eyes till I say."

So they both shut their eyes. It looks funny, like they're praying for me, or they're those people on *Changing Rooms* waiting to see what Laurence Llewelyn-Bowen's done to their house.

I manage to start peeing and then hold the stick in the stream. Then I sit down to stare at the test. After a couple of minutes (the longest of my life) a thin blue line starts to appear. I nearly scream out loud but bite my lip. The girls have still got their eyes shut.

"Can we look yet?" goes Shel.

"No!" I snap.

I will the blue line to fade away again. I blink hard in case the staring has made my eyes go funny. But it's still there, strong and clear now. Oh. My. God. "I'm pregnant," I murmur.

Shel and Jen's eyes snap open. "Oh, Lia!" cries Jen, lungeing over to hug me.

Shelley takes the stick from my hand and squints at it, then checks the instructions. "No, you're not," she says.

What? "But you said the blue line. . ."

"This is just the test line, to show it's working. There's no second blue line. You're not pregnant."

Jen sighs deeply and slides down on to the floor. "Jeeeeez! Thank God for that. I was so worried."

"Now you can tell that arsehole Jase to get stuffed," says Shelley.

I do the other test – just to make sure – and there's no second blue line on that one either. I'm so relieved I can't even think, let alone speak. It's like I've been handed my life back. I get what people mean now, when they say *flooded with relief.* It's like a drug in your veins. We're all sitting here, just sort of bewildered, when the phone rings.

Jen goes to get it while I chuck the test out and wash my hands. Then me and Shel go up too. When we get into Jen's room, she's talking into the receiver in a low whisper. "Look, just leave her alone, OK? It's none of your business whether she is or not. Not after the way you've treated her."

She turns round and I motion for her to give me the phone. She's shaking her head, but I take it off her and hear, ". . .and I know what you think of me but this is between me and Lia so just put her on the bloody phone, all right?"

"Jase, it's me," I say, very quietly.

"Lia. Thank God."

"Has Hazel gone?"

Jase sounds put out. "Hazel? What are you on about?"

I sigh. "Jase, don't give me any bullshit. Not now, OK?"

Jase pauses, then, "She's gone. I got rid of her straight after. . . After you rang I mean, not. . . Oh, shit, look, Li, I didn't mean to sound harsh, but you don't want a baby either, not at your age. You want to do training and. . ."

"It was negative."

There's a deep sigh. "Thank fuck for that."

Strangely, I feel hurt that he's so relieved, even though I am too. "But we still need to talk," I say, keeping my voice low and quiet, so I can hold it steady. "About me and you."

"OK. Look, Mum's out all day. Come round now, yeah? Just give me half an hour to shower and that."

There's an awkward silence where we're both thinking, *shower, change the sheets, empty the ashtray*. In short, get rid of *her*. But neither of us says anything.

"Fine, see you then." And I hang up.

When I turn round the girls are staring at me like I've been replaced by a blue alien from the Planet Mug.

"You're not actually going round there?" says Jen.

"There's stuff to sort out," I say.

"After what he did with Hazel?" asks Shel. "Come on,

255

Lia. Wake up and smell the complete bastard."

I don't blame them. How can they possibly understand how it is with me and Jase? "The Hazel thing's bad, sure, but hey, people get drunk, people get stupid. I need to see him, to talk it over. There's a lot between us."

"Lia, please don't. . ." says Jen.

"I'm going round there in half an hour," I tell them. "So either you can be supportive and drive me over there or you can stay here and bitch about what an idiot I am."

They get on my side then, when they see I won't budge. So I have a shower and borrow a pair of black jeans and a hoodie from Jen. Shel drives me over there, with Jen sitting lengthways on the tiny back seat.

We park up round the corner from Brambles' drive.

"Thanks for the ride. You don't have to wait," I say.

"We will," says Shel. She looks really determined so I don't argue. They'll get bored after a while and head home.

I walk up the drive and Jase opens the door before I even ring the bell. He pulls me close, swirling me into his peppermint-smoke-Lacoste smell, his hands wrapped round my hips. I feel my body whirring into life at his touch. There's something between us I can't explain. I think we'd know each other even in the dark. Even after fifty years.

But I pull away. This isn't just about sex any more. "You were still seeing her!"

"Shush!" Jase pulls me in and shuts the door behind us.

I realize he's hushing me up 'cause there are Brambles volunteers about. *Girls like me.* He leads me into the living room, sits me down, gets me a glass of water without asking, like I've had a shock.

"You were still seeing her," I repeat, as he tries to hand me the glass that I won't take. I watch it slip through my limp fingers and he has to grab it to stop it dropping on the carpet.

"Just last night, I swear. I got pissed up and made a mistake. But it won't happen again. She's too much like hard work."

I arch my eyebrow. "And I'm not?"

"Oh, come on, Li. I didn't mean it like that. You said yourself you're not into all the emotional bollocks. We're two of a kind."

"There's no way I'm two of a kind with *you*," I say flatly. "I'd never talk like that about a *baby*, for God's sake, like it's a bit of rubbish you can just throw away."

He sits down next to me and puts his arm around me. I know I should shrug it off, but I don't want to react, so I just let it dangle there. "I didn't mean to sound . . . you know. I was just, like – *whoa*!"

I finally look at him. His gorgeous sandy hair. His

257

piercing blue eyes. I get hot shivers all up my body. "Yeah, sure. I don't blame you."

"Great." He squeezes my shoulder and leans in to kiss me but I turn away.

"I mean, what else could I expect from such a spineless bastard?"

Jase blinks at me. He obviously thought he was on the home straight. Quick apology, and back together, in bed within half an hour. He looks like he's about to get in a huff, but then he smiles. It's as if I can see his thoughts like big cartoon bubbles floating over his head, *keep her sweet, shame to waste an empty house.*

"This is why we're so good together," he says. "You're the only person who can stand up to me. Look, this time we'll do it properly. No more messing about with Hazel. Just you and me. I want you to be my *girlfriend.*"

Girlfriend. He says it like this big reward, this big bribe. If I'm a good girl. . .

Thinking about it, I realize that he's never called me his girlfriend, and only once asked me round here. We meet in the pub or the park. I don't call the house phone. Suddenly a whole lot of things fall into place.

I'm not the girl he cheated *on* – I'm the girl he cheated *with.*

"I thought we understood each other's feelings without having to say anything," I say, holding my voice steady, "but all the time you were just keeping your options open. Don't pretend that's the first time you've slept with Hazel either. You never really split up with her. In fact, you're probably just giving me the girlfriend line now 'cause she dumped you when I rang."

Jase gives me a freaked out look, like, *how the hell are you doing this?* But I haven't suddenly come over all Mystic Meg. It's just that Jase's mind is a textbook cliché – a five-year-old could read it.

"I never said we were going out," he says. Hmm, the case for the defence.

"True," I concede.

"But come on, how about we give it a go? Just me and you."

I smile. He gazes at me, then smiles too, slow and sexy.

"OK," I say.

He moves to kiss me and this time I let him. He pushes me down into the sofa in a really serious snog and it's wonderful, amazing, feeling my boobs pressed up against his chest, my hands grabbing his shoulders. When we finally break apart, we're both gasping, so turned on it hurts.

"Oh, excellent. You won't regret this, Lia. Honestly, from now on. . . I'll just get. . . You know. . . Won't be a sec." Jase stumbles upstairs.

I smile and let him go. I don't want a scene at the door when I get up and walk out of it. Jase might have thought that was a kiss hello, but really it was a kiss goodbye.

Before, I was so devastated I couldn't feel anything. I was shocked numb. But I've found my fury now. It swirls inside me like an electric storm, twitching and buzzing. Thank God for this crackling surge of rage. It's the only thing strong enough to tear me away from here, from *him*.

I slip out and then I run – just to feel my heart pounding, my feet banging on the gravel driveway, my freedom. I remember the last time I bolted down this driveway, red-faced and totally gutted about Jase and Hazel. Hot tears slide down my cheeks and I cry out with pain that this time he wants me, but I'm still running. I nearly stop, and turn, but my anger drives me on. However much I want him, there's no going back. Not after this.

I remember how last time I wished I had a hot date in a Ferrari round the corner. I realize now I've got something better, a recon MGB with two mates in it – OK, so one's on another planet and the other's a bossy control freak, but they both love me to bits. I wouldn't swap them for the world. I pound up to the car and throw myself in. Shel hugs me, her face half-covered by her huge especially-for-monster-hangovers sunglasses. Jen puts her hand on my shoulder from the back seat. "Good for you, Lia," she says. "You didn't stay."

I wipe my eyes on my sleeve. "Nah, I know what's good for me. Plus, you two are better than a hot date in a Ferrari any day . . . in a non-sexual way, obviously."

They both give me puzzled looks.

"Oh, forget it."

Just then, Jase comes pounding round the corner and spots the car. He looks at me with a mixed expression on his face – hurt, yes, but anger too – like we had a deal and I broke it. He comes striding up to the car.

"Step on it!" I yell, and Shel puts her foot down and hares off the kerb, going a bit closer to Jase than strictly necessary, making him jump out of the way.

"Shelley!" Jen shrieks.

"Yee-hah!" shouts Shel. "Make way for the goddess-mobile!"

We get some bacon and egg sarnies and a bottle of orange juice in Sainsbury's and go and sit in Kelsey Park. We could all do with the fresh air.

When we've had our little picnic and I've finished feeding bits of bread to the birds, we go for a walk round the ponds, linking arms. I skip a step so I'm walking with the same foot as them. It's such a good feeling, striding along like that. Every so often the sun peeks out from behind a cloud and heat soaks into us. We stop and watch the Canada geese on the big pond, and the little kids going up and down on plastic trikes.

"Fancy coming over to watch a film?" I say.

"Actually, I've got to get home," says Jen. "There's

something I want to do and if I leave it I might change my mind."

"What are you talking about?" asks Shel.

"I'm going to pack up the dressing table, like Lia suggested."

I feel really bad, like what I said has shamed her into doing it. "Jen, are you sure?"

"Absolutely. I mean, they're just things, aren't they? Very precious things maybe, but they're not her and they're not me. I want to let them go. I can't explain it, but I just don't feel like I need them any more. I feel better. Not *guilty*. Thinking about it now, it must have been the thing about the shoes. Maybe I thought it was my fault she died – because I couldn't get the second one off."

I don't know what to say, so I just smile at her. Shel doesn't say anything either, but she's smiling too. I reckon Jen knows how proud of her we are.

"How about you, Shel?" I ask.

"Thanks but I want to get home too. I've got to face Mum sometime. Plus, I need a bath and a kip. There's that Nines gig tonight."

"Oh, yeah. Are you going with Stick?" I say, before I remember what happened. Christ, my gob is like a deadly weapon. Maybe I could get it surgically removed on the NHS.

Shel just shrugs. "Maybe. Come on, let's go."

22

"The Love Magician strikes again."

Mum doesn't even look surprised when I say I'm moving out. "This is about Paul, isn't it?"

It would be so easy to say yes, but I reckon I owe her an honest explanation. "Not about *him*, no, but about what it means when a guy comes round here to pick me up and you sleep with him."

"Well, what was I supposed to do?" she asks, eyes twinkling.

She's trying to get me to laugh. Instead, I nearly choke. "Mum! Most people's parents can usually manage to get their daughter's date a cup of tea without stripping off and shagging him!"

She looks at me with her head on one side. "You have *seen* him, right? There's no way I'm putting the kettle on when. . ."

So, she's obviously not going to apologize or anything, then. She always tries to joke about things that have upset me, to bring me round. She honestly believes I'm just sulking because I lost this particular game. But it's more than that – I don't want to play any more. I don't want her competing with me – over anything. And I shouldn't have bothered trying to explain, either. Mum's better on facts than feelings.

"I'll start looking for a place this weekend," I say, focussing on the practical stuff. "And I'll pay you rent till I find somewhere."

She goes all small and vulnerable then, pulling her knees up to her chest on the kitchen chair and tucking in her dressing gown round her feet. "Shel, don't talk like that."

"Mum, I know it's the right thing to do."

"Look, sorry for joking about it. And, well, sorry for doing it. I didn't realize how much you liked him." I want to tell her I didn't really like him, that she's totally missing the point, but she keeps talking. "We can spend more time together. Do girly stuff. Double dates. Shopping."

But she's dangled this carrot in front of me before. It lasts about a week and then she's back off with The Witches and wrapped up in one of her boring married men. So I know I've got to hold firm. "Mum, I don't need another mate. I've got Jen and Lia for that."

She snorts, like *what possible use are they?* but resists saying it. "Running your own house isn't that simple, Shelley. There'll be all the cleaning and maintenance to do and getting workmen in when something goes wrong. You have to watch them, you know, or they rip you off."

I can't help smirking at that one. Mum held our plumber's wrench for him on several occasions, until his marriage sprang a leak and he got into deep water.

"Home-ownership's no joke, young lady," she says, going all mature on me. "There are the bills to organize and. . ."

"Mum, I've been running our finances since I was fourteen. My only worry is that you won't understand the system when I'm gone."

She looks me right in the eye. "Shel, please don't go. You're all I've got."

Ouch, she's deployed her most effective stealth weapon – emotional blackmail – like something deadly that drops from the sky while you're not looking. But I can't let her manipulate me. Not any more. It's been the pattern of our whole life together. If I take a step backwards, away from her, she comes forward, but as soon as I step forward she steps back. It's not motherly love, it's ballroom dancing.

"I'm going to look at those new designer flats coming up in Manor Road," I say, focussing on the detail so I don't crack up and back down.

"Very posh. My house not good enough for you, now?"

"Mum, you know that's not why I'm going. Besides, you can close up the internal door and rent my place out as a studio flat. You'd get a nice bit of cash."

She pouts. "I don't want strangers in the house, I want you."

I really want to believe her. But we've been here before. It's time to face facts. "Mum, we *are* strangers."

That's it. She won't look at me now. She just stares at the opposite wall, zoned out.

"About that rent," I say. "I'll find out the going rate and pay you that till I move out."

I know she won't talk any more so I grab the free paper off her kitchen table, run upstairs to my flat and shut the door. I flop on to my sofa and rifle through the pages. I call Proctors, and after getting a ballpark rent estimate for this place I ask about those apartments in Manor Road. I make an appointment to view them on Saturday morning at nine. Then I go and lie on my bed but I can't sleep, my mind's churning too much. But not about Mum, or Lia, or Jen.

About Stick.

I don't want to give up on us, but he's made it clear he's not interested. And if I want to move on, I guess I'm going to have to let him go.

And I know how to do it, too.

I run a bath and lie there with my eyes closed, imagining all the possible ways it could go, like where he tells me never to darken his doorstep again. I torture myself imagining a few of the impossible ways too, like where he says he loves me and wants me back. Then I put on my really gorgeous plain grey bias-cut dress from Kew, and my black Kookster shoes. I don't wear them much 'cause normally they feel too clunky on my big feet, but clunky's what I want now. I'm hoping they'll weigh me down to earth and help me do this.

I shake my hair out and leave it loose. No make-up, no jewellery, no perfume. I feel like a piece of driftwood stripped bare by the sea and I guess I want to look like it too. Like just me, the way I am underneath.

I pull my Nines ticket off from where it's blu-tacked to my mirror.

I walk to Stick's, not along the high street but the back way, down leafy residential roads full of new-build blocks of flats and conversions. I trail my hand along walls and hedges as I go, wishing I could leave a line of breadcrumbs to get back safely. I'm going out on a limb here, and I'm not used to feeling so out of control.

I get on to Stick's tree-lined street, Kings Hall Road, where it's big comfortable Victorian semis, covered in vines and wisteria, behind slightly shaggy front lawns. I clunk up his drive and nearly ring the front bell, but suddenly I don't want Sophia or Christopher to answer it, so I creep round the side to his window. My stomach flips thinking about the last time I stood here, about to climb through, and all the good things that came after. But I can't think about *that*, or it'll be impossible to do *this*.

Stick's in there nodding away with headphones on whilst tapping stuff into his computer, and I wave at the window till he notices me. He opens it and looks at me warily, like I'm going to climb in and whip my clothes off again. "Hey, Shel, you are allowed round the front, you know," he says.

"Thanks, but I'm not staying." I hand him my ticket. "Here, look after this for me."

Stick tries to hand it back but I wave it away. "But if I don't come you won't be able to get in."

I shuffle awkwardly, glad of my clunky shoes sticking me to the spot. "Look, I know I'm not *someone*, but . . . we always go together. So I was hoping we could tonight . . . as mates, yeah? I'll be at the Lily."

It's breaking my heart, not to mention what it's doing to my rude bits, but I love Stick, and if friendship is what he wants, then that's what I'm going to give him. I walk away quickly, before he can say anything, because to be honest I'm scared he'll tell me he doesn't even want *that* any more.

I stride up to the Lily and sit over a cappuccino, working it out in my head. It's half five now. The gig's at half seven, so if he's coming we need to get on the train by six thirty. So he's got an hour to get here, or I'll know he doesn't want to hang out with me any more. This way, if he doesn't, he won't have to say it and I won't have to hear it. Ingenious plan, huh?

Tony puts on a CD, Norah Jones singing "Don't

Know Why". The music reminds me of our first night together. Tony can't know that – but he must know I'm waiting for Stick. I've been looking up from the G2 section I'm pretending to read every time the bell goes over the door. It's ticking up to quarter past six. The other customers have gone and he's sweeping around and putting chairs on tables. He'll shut at half past. Stick knows that, too.

Twenty-five past. I feel sick. I really thought he'd come. OK, so he's not going to be with me, I accept that. But is he going to ditch our friendship as well?

Half past. *Apparently he is.*

Tony gives me a sympathetic smile as I murmur "bye" and get up to go. It's as though I've done my penance spending an agonizing hour sitting here waiting for Stick to show, and he's forgiven me for what happened before. I leave a nice tip on the table, 'cause I don't think I'll be in for a while.

I'm heading out the door, staring at the floor as my eyes fill with more bloody tears, and I bang right into someone. I mutter "sorry" without looking up.

"Shel?"

Stick grabs me and kisses me, right in the doorway. It's incredible – amazing – and we only break apart when the wholesale man needs to get in to deliver a catering-size box of ketchup sachets.

I just stare at him, totally bewildered. "But you said. . ."

"What did I know," he says, squeezing my shoulders, touching my hair, making me feel full of magic, like the greatest Love Goddess ever.

I wish I could just let things be. But I have to say it, don't I? I have to know. "But I thought you just wanted to be mates?"

"Yeah."

"Well, I hate to break it to you, but if this is how you are with your friends, you should probably change schools."

Stick smiles and kisses me again. "With the ticket thing, I realized you'd put what I wanted first, even though it isn't what you wanted. Then I worked out that I wanted what you wanted after all and I wanted to give you what you wanted too."

I peer at him. "Nope – didn't get any of that," I say, and we both laugh awkwardly.

"Doesn't matter. Just as long as we're back on, yeah?"

"Course we're back on," I say. Yes! I never thought this could happen and it has. I've got him back. It's my best impossible scenario come true.

Stick sits down at his favourite table and I take my usual place opposite him. Tony's grinning as he puts two cappuccinos down in front of us. "Cheers, Tone," says Stick. He takes both Nines tickets out of his pocket and hands them over. "Here you go, mate. Take Lily out."

Tony takes the tickets and squints at them. "You sure?"

"Yeah, we need a bit of time."

"Excellent. Cheers, mate." Tony gives him the keys to lock up and then vanishes upstairs.

We sit holding hands across the table, sipping our coffees, smiling awkwardly at each other. This is the table we had the maybe-kiss at and it's also the one we broke up at.

Thinking about that, I feel those crazy fears rising again. Fear of it working out, of this being it. But this time I decide to be honest about it. "Stick, I'm worried about us getting back together. What if. . .?"

I sit here hardly breathing, scared there's going to be a repeat of the break up, that he'll be furious I'm having doubts straight away. But he just smiles. "Life's not like in films, Shel. It doesn't end two minutes after the couple gets together. I'm wondering if getting involved is sensible too. But who wants to be sensible? Maybe we're never going to be sure. Still, we can be not sure together."

I sigh with relief. Thank God, room to be not sure. That's all I ever wanted, I just didn't know it. "Stick," I say, leaning towards him over the table, "I lo—"

But he puts a finger to my lips. "Don't say it, Shel. Let's save something."

About five minutes later, Tony and Lily come back through and head out the door.

"See you later."

"Yeah, have a good night."

"You too."

Tony's eyes slide to the door of their flat and Stick's follow. He's left it on the latch. Lily winks at me and I smile back. When they've gone I look at Stick and I want him so much I wonder if we'll even make it up the stairs. He stands up, pulling on my hand. But my crazy stupid brain is obviously not connected to the rest of my body, because there's something I just have to know, and it won't wait.

"Stick, can I ask you something?"

He bobs back down, half hovering over his chair. "Sure."

"You know that time in here when I'd just quit school and you kind of leaned over the table and . . . well . . . were you just going to wipe chocolate powder off my cheek, or. . ."

"Let me think," he says, teasing, smiling. "No, I believe I was going to do this."

He kisses me, long and slow and deep. "Mmm," I say, when we finally break apart. "The Love Magician strikes again."

And no, we don't make it up the stairs.

23

"Life's full of surprises. That's my new mantra."

 I smooth down the front of the black lycra shirt that's been lurking in the back of my wardrobe for the last six months. "Are you sure it doesn't make the top of my arms look fat?"

Shelley laughs. "Course not. It's really sexy. You can even borrow my Valentinos again if you want."

"Thanks, but I'll wear these," I say, stepping into the Rocket Dogs I bought with Nan's birthday money. They're really cool – pink sandals with a wedgie candy stripe heel.

"Oh, wow, Jen, they're so *you*."

"Thanks. Hey, why are you offering me swishy shoes anyway? It's only the cinema." *And you wouldn't if you knew about the broken heel*, I think, smiling as I remember Nicola Start, my knight in shining lycra.

"Oh, because it's your birthday, that's all." Shelley flips her phone open and glances at the time. "Ready?"

"Yeah, just let me sort my hair out."

"Ah, my old proverb: get the hair right and

273

everything else will follow. Even if no one is going to see it."

I automatically go to straighten my hair but then I decide to make the most of the curl and scrunch it up. I have to admit it looks good, and I think maybe it can be part of the new me, the me who isn't trying to be like Mum. I hope Shelley's proverb is true, that if I get the hair right, the rest of the new me will follow.

I'm just experimenting with some glittery slides when Shelley gets all impatient and marches me down the stairs. I say a quick goodbye to Nan as she virtually drags me out of the house and makes for her car.

"What's the rush? The film doesn't start till half eight. Come on, let's walk."

But Shelley hovers by the car door. "Do you mind if we drive? I need to pop into the Lily first. Stick wanted me to pick up some records for him."

"But Tony'll be shut now, surely. . ."

"Erm, yeah, but he's given me a key for . . . you know, these type of emergencies."

I give up and get in the car. There's no arguing with Shelley.

We park up outside the Lily Pad and she unlocks the door and turns the lights on. All these people pop out from behind the counter and yell, "Surprise!"

I blink at them, then at the balloons and streamers strung round the café. It takes a minute to

274

realize it's all for me. I start laughing and crying at once and everyone claps and launches into a shambolical rendition of "Happy Birthday". Lia's here, and Stick and some mates from his school, Carrie, Lucy and that lot from ours plus their upper sixth boyfriends, the bunch from my English class and some of Dylan's Brit School mates.

I just keep staring. I still can't believe it's all for me. "Thanks!" I manage to croak, as they all start cheering again.

Someone gets the music going and Shelley grabs us both a drink from the table piled with cans and bottles. Lia comes up, a bottle of her favourite vodka mix in her hand.

"Is it OK?" she says nervously. "I know you don't like surprises."

I give her a big hug, and then pull Shelley in too. "Happy tears – honest. It's brilliant. Life's *full* of surprises. I'm just getting used to it. But hey, where are Tony and Lily?"

"Out. They don't want to know anything about under-age drinking."

I frown. "They don't *mind*, do they?"

"Oh, no," says Shelley. "Tony was handing me a corkscrew and a bottle opener when he said it."

Just then Dylan walks in with this woman. I stare and then realize and look away quickly. It's The Blond. Yeah, seriously. He comes up and says, "Hi, I'm Nicky.

Happy Birthday. Ooh, I love the way you've done your hair."

I kiss him, sorry, *her*, on both cheeks. Then she excuses herself to "freshen up". Shelley and Lia say hi to Dylan then slide off, presumably to hide in a corner and go, *Did you see that bloke? Oh. My. God.* Dylan puts his guitar carefully down and pulls me into a huge hug. "Happy Birthday, Angel."

"Thanks." I hand him a tinny and he cracks it open and drinks half of it down in one go.

"I need this," he says. "He's only been living as a woman for one week and already he's developed this complete obsession with hair and make-up!"

"We're not all like that, you know," I say, pretend-offended. I'm glad he didn't see me getting ready tonight, though. Like with the Shelley's mum horror story, I stay cool, acting like this sort of thing happens to me all the time. "So, Nick's Nicky now, huh?"

Dylan groans. "Typical, isn't it? I come out and get this great boyfriend and then he announces he wants to be a woman."

I nearly choke on my OJ, not sure whether to laugh or cry or both. "So you've split up, then?"

Dylan gives me a look, like, *duh*, and I say, "I'll take that as a yes."

"It's OK, you can laugh. I see the irony, but it's also like . . . *bollocks*. I really liked Nick as Nick. I'm still getting over it."

"Yeah, it's not easy when you want to be with someone but there's an unchangeable thing inside them that means you can't. Takes a bit of getting used to."

Dylan gives me this intense look. "Spot on. How come you know so much about it?"

"Oh, I had a thing for this gay guy once."

He smiles, getting my drift, and squeezes my hand gently. "I'm so sorry, Jen."

I lean into him, resting my head on his shoulder. "No need, really. I'm OK. And you will be too. You just need to let go and move on."

"Is that what you're doing?"

"Yeah."

"Well then that's what I'll do too." He scans the room. "Hmm, what about that guy over there?"

"That's Stick's mate Marcus. And FYI I saw him first."

Dylan laughs deeply, throwing his head back to swig more beer. "You go, girl! Hey, listen, I sent the demo off to some indie labels. A guy from Transound rang up and said he might pop in later to hear me play. Shouldn't think he will, though."

"You never know. Life's full of surprises. That's my new mantra." I smile at him, and grab a bottle of beer from the table. "Now, if you'll excuse me, I've noticed Marcus has finished his drink."

I wink at him and swish off to give Marcus the beer

and have a chat. Smooth or what? Apparently the new me has a bit of confidence too. Course I'm not over Dylan and I'm not up for getting together with anyone else yet, but there's no law against window shopping, is there?

After a while, Stick disentangles himself from Shelley and heads over to our posse, so I go back over to her, collecting another birthday hug on the way (I totally understand what she sees in him!). We chat as I give her a hand putting more crisps in bowls. She tells me about moving out and I get worried about her going too far away, but she promises me she'll be well within tea and biccies distance. In fact, she's thinking of Manor Road.

"Have you done your cards yet?" she says.

I'm touched because I know Shelley thinks tarot reading is a load of rubbish. I've done a "the year ahead" reading on my birthday for the last four years, ever since I got into the new age stuff. But I didn't do it today. It's not that I've stopped believing in it, no way. I just don't feel like I need to know right now. "Not this year," I say. "I think I'll just take the future as it comes."

"Me too," she says, smiling mysteriously.

"Meaning?"

She does the famous Shelley shrug. "Oh, nothing."

"Come on, spill. It's *my* party, so you have to tell me."

She smiles. "I wasn't going to mention it yet, but . . . Stick might move in when I get my new place, see how it goes. We've got an idea for a film script. We might write it together, then maybe try and get some funding."

"I thought he was going to uni?"

"He's having a year out first. And like I said, we're seeing how it goes. He's got a conditional place at Brighton but what with the Love Magician and the film and all that. . ."

I give her a stern look and she says, "Don't worry, we'll both get back to it, one day."

But I really wonder. Now they're together, working on their own stuff, Shelley and Stick don't seem to need any other anchors in life. And maybe it's the right thing for them. As for me, I'm glad I've got another year at school, and with Nan, before I have to think about anything big like that.

Lia comes up and starts helping us put the bowls out. "Thanks again for organizing this," I say.

"No probs."

"How are things with your parents now?"

"Yeah, fine. I haven't told them about the scare, though. It'd probably give Dad a heart attack. I came on yesterday, thank God. I know we did the test, but I've never been so happy to see my period in my life! And Mum and Dad were really sweet about Jase in the end. Mum even said he could stay over if I wanted. She reckoned they'd rather we're at home, where they know I'm safe, than out doing it in a car somewhere. But I told her we broke up."

"You're still OK about that?" asks Shelley.

"Yeah. Ancient history. Just don't ever get me drunk and leave me alone with him 'cause I wouldn't be responsible for my actions. Oh, hey, it was so nice – Mum and I had this big girly chat and she told me about her first time."

Shelley smiles kind of sadly. "That's lovely. I wish me and Mum could be like that."

"Try living with my nan," I say. "I wish she'd stop talking about her and Grandad's, you know, *love* life. Eeeek! But I wouldn't change her. She's a one off."

Lia giggles. "Well, it would have been really sweet if it hadn't been with my *dad*. I've hardly been able to look him in the eye since!"

She leans over to get the last raspberry vodka and I notice the black lace thong sticking out of the back of her combats. "You're wearing your Goddess-Society-Approved Underwear then?"

"Yeah. I'm giving up blokes for a while, got to knuckle down at school, you know. So the sexy underwear's having a final outing."

"I'm wearing mine too," says Shelley, reaching into her hipster flares and producing a sliver of purple lace. Stick glances over and goes silent in mid-sentence, making us all giggle.

"Me too," I say. "I'm not showing you, though."

"You never know, Jen," Shelley says, letting go of the sliver so it pings out of sight. "Marcus obviously fancies you. Tonight could be the night."

"Nah, I'm not ready to get into anything yet. Seriously, girls, I think this should be the end of the society. It's been great, but I'm really OK with being a virgin now. The last thing I want is pressure to lose it."

I think they're going to say no again, and insist we're all in it till we're all not. But they don't. They seem to understand that I really mean it now.

"OK," says Shelley. "One last toast. To the Goddess Society."

We all clink bottles. "The Goddess Society."

Just then a stocky blond lad comes in with an older guy. I assume they're together, but then, watching them, they don't seem to know each other. The boy glances shyly around, as the man, who looks totally at home, helps himself to a drink. Lia follows my gaze and clocks them. "Oh my God, Jack's here! Do I look all right?"

"Stunning. Let me just. . ." I scan her slash-front Punky Fish top and do up the zip that goes right across her cleavage. "That's better. Anyway, who's Jack? I thought you were off guys?"

"I am," says Lia, raising her eyebrow at me and undoing the zip again. "But I couldn't miss out on Jack. He's too lush. I met him at the RSPCA place I've

281

volunteered at. I'm not going back to Brambles."

"He's a bit old, Lia. Even by your standards."

But she just smiles and calls out, "Hey, Jack!"

The boy turns and grins as she hurries across the café and hugs him. Then she leans over the table to get him a drink, making sure he gets the full effect of the thong. Chatting away, she pulls him over and introduces us. Jack says Happy Birthday and gives me a present, some gorgeous moonstone earrings, which is really sweet seeing as he's never even met me before.

"Who's the other guy?" I ask Shelley.

She peers at him, taking in the battered leather jacket, stubble, grey fleece. "Dunno."

The little boho-looking posse from the Brit School start shouting, "Dylan! Dylan!" and it dawns on me that the mystery guy is from Transound. Dylan gets his guitar out, sits on the edge of one of the tables and does a couple of his songs – one from the demo and a new one. They're really good and he gets a massive clap and cheer after each one. The Transound guy's smiling and nodding along. He looks pretty impressed.

Then Dylan says, "This one's for a very good friend of mine," and winks at me. I go instantly red but I forget to be embarrassed after a while, 'cause the song's so beautiful.

"There are only two ways to get out of this world
For a girl who's afraid to let go

She'll crawl through the mirror
Or lay on the tracks
And both ways she's leaving alone.
But I don't want you to be crazy or dead
There's got to be somewhere else to go
Somewhere to send all the thoughts in your head
Some way to carry you home
Am I getting through –
Am I getting through –
To you?"

Dylan's smiling, singing straight to me. *We're not in love. We're not lovers. But we love each other, and that's better than anything else.* That's freedom. But then, maybe freedom can mean different things.

I watch Shelley leaning against Stick, swaying to the music, his black-nail-varnished hands wrapped round her tiny waist. Maybe freedom can mean committing to something, even though it scares you.

I watch Lia's hand reaching for Jack's as they stand listening, his fingers looped around hers. Maybe freedom can mean cutting your losses and starting again.

To me, now, freedom means simply letting go. Not just of Dylan, but of Mum too. I have to step out of her shadow, her shoes, well, shoe. Of course, I won't forget her. I still think she's close by in some way, helping me out.

But I know a mirror is just a mirror.

So there you have it. The whole story of the Goddess Society. I'm still finding out who I am, and I probably will be for ever, but I've made a start and, for now, that's good enough. And as for being a virgin, so what? I'll meet another The One – all in good time.

The song, my song, ends and everyone claps and cheers for Dylan. Wired, he launches into the middle of "Freedom". Everyone starts jumping up and down, belting it out. I let Shelley and Lia pull me into the dancing crowd and I join in too. I can't stop grinning. I'm with my best friends, at my surprise birthday party, dancing in my own shoes. I'm not a Barbie doll, I wouldn't want to be, but, for the first time in my life, I actually feel like a goddess.